THE INEXPLICABLE LOVE

EMBRACING MISERY TOGETHER

EKTA

Made with ♥ on the Notion Press Platform

www.notionpress.com

With heartfelt gratitude, I extend my sincere thanks to my family. Your unwavering support and encouragement have been the driving force behind bringing this book to life. Your belief in me and insistence on taking my writing seriously have transformed a mere hobby into a published work. Thank you for inspiring me to share my passion rather than keep it hidden. This book is a testament to the love and encouragement that surrounds me, and I am profoundly grateful for each of you who played a role in making this journey possible.

This book is specially dedicated to my father, the unsung hero behind my stellar school essay grades. Thanks for ghostwriting those essays, Papa! Your secret's safe with me... and now the world knows who the real literary genius in the family is!

Contents

Contents

Contents

Preface

Love is a paradox—a force that can be as uplifting as it is confounding, as beautiful as it is devastating. In *The Inexplicable Love*, we delve into a world where the lines between devotion and desire blur, where the past refuses to let go, and the present demands answers that the heart may not be ready to give.

This is the story of Nikita, a woman caught in the crossfire of love, friendship, care and betrayals. Her journey is not a linear path but a winding road filled with choices that challenge her sense of self, her values, and her definition of love.

Through her struggles, *The Inexplicable Love* explores universal questions: Can we ever truly move on from our past? Is love a choice, or is it something that chooses us? And when the heart is torn, how do we decide what deserves to be held onto and what must be let go?

This story is not about heroes or villains, but about deeply flawed, deeply human characters trying to navigate the complexities of their emotions. It's about the battles we fight within ourselves—the pull of nostalgia, the weight of promises, and the longing for a love that feels complete.

As you turn these pages, I invite you to step into Nikita's shoes, to feel her turmoil, and to question along with her the meaning of love and loyalty. This book is not about finding the "right" answer but about embracing the uncertainty and growth that love brings.

Welcome to *The Inexplicable Love.*

Foreword

The Inexplicable Love is a story about choices, regret, passion, and the messy, tangled web of human emotions. It is a deep dive into the essence of relationships—how they shape us, break us, and sometimes rebuild us in the most unexpected ways. It's about a woman navigating the choppy waters of love, weighed down by her own insecurities, past mistakes, and the unrelenting pressure of expectations. In her journey, she discovers that love is not always logical, that it can defy reason and explanation, leaving us vulnerable yet more alive than ever before.

This story is for anyone who has ever struggled with the ghosts of the past and the promises of the present. It's for those who've wrestled with doubt, guilt, and the longing to feel whole. Through its pages, we are reminded that love is never as simple as it seems, but it's always worth fighting for—even when the fight is with ourselves.

I hope *The Inexplicable Love* resonates with you, not just as a tale of romantic entanglement but as a mirror reflecting the complexities of human connection. May it remind you that while love might be inexplicable, it is always transformative.

Prologue

Beneath the polished veneer of office professionalism, power plays and personal vendettas thrived. For Nikita, a fresh-faced MBA graduate, this world was both intimidating and intriguing—a battlefield she had yet to conquer.

Her days were a predictable loop of scoldings, piled-up assignments, and judgmental glances, mostly from her boss, Rajeev. To everyone else, he was Mr. Arrogant, a man with an icy demeanor and a sharp tongue who ruled the office with an iron fist. For Nikita, he was an enigma—someone she despised yet oddly respected for treating her as an equal.

Then there were Rahul and Priya, her childhood friends, who could always find a way to make her forget her office troubles and laugh, even on her worst days. But Rahul and Priya had their own set of secrets and dramas hidden from Nikita, waiting to unfold.

Each character played their part in a story far more intricate than it appeared—a story of ambition, betrayal, and unexpected alliances.

Welcome to The Inexplicable Love, where the line between personal and professional is blurred, as the characters find themselves entangled in a web of power and vulnerability, where loyalty will be tested and intentions will be questioned.

Acknowledgements

I gratefully acknowledge my husband, Rishabh, for his exceptional support and invaluable contribution to this book. His meticulous editing have significantly elevated its quality, transforming it into something truly remarkable. Thank you for your unwavering commitment and insightful contributions, which have made this work truly special.

ONE
THEY MEET

"Oh damn, new interns again! Why don't we just hire people with some experience?" thought Rajeev as he bumped into an intern while entering the lift. As he looked at her clumsily picking up her bag and files, he thought, "Now they have stopped bothering to come to the office groomed! The shabby dress is at least taking attention away from her no-makeup face. Did she just wake up and come here? Has she even combed her hair? College kids these days! No idea about professional dressing sense." The elevator opened, and he walked off towards his cabin, leaving the intern still fumbling with her things on the ground.

Nikita was late to her first day, a day she had been eagerly anticipating as it marked her debut in the corporate world, especially considering she was surprised to secure a position at a prestigious company like ST Consultancy. Her timid and introverted demeanor hadn't been favorable in previous interviews, leading to multiple rejections. However, perhaps her unwavering determination was recognized by her almost 50th interviewer, or maybe he simply felt generous; regardless, she landed the job. She was determined not to disappoint her interviewer or give him any reason to doubt his decision, but the relentless Mumbai traffic refused to allow her even a moment's respite.

She stumbled into the elevator, her files scattering across the floor, alongside an arrogant man who didn't bother to help pick up even a single piece of paper. "Never mind," she thought. "I don't need special treatment as a girl. I will prove to them that they have hired the best." After finally gathering everything, she reached the HR floor to understand her work, only to be directed to another floor. "Everyone seems too busy. Maybe it's a good thing; they might not notice my clumsiness and late entry at all," Nikita thought optimistically. However, her smile vanished when she saw her mentor for the new job – Mr. Arrogant, the guy from the elevator.

Nikita, already timid, reached a whole new level of nervousness upon encountering Mr. Arrogant, her stammering intensifying. "I... was... HR sent me... I have joined today... with you," she managed to stutter out a few words. Rajeev couldn't grasp what she was saying and became convinced she was even more incompetent than he had initially thought. He directed her to sit in the cubicle outside his office and instructed her to contact IT for setting up her system until he assigned her a project. Nikita attempted to gather courage and asked again, "Where is IT?" Rajeev, reaching his limit, shouted, "Get HR to babysit you; I don't have time for this!" Nikita felt her already fragile self-confidence shatter, but as she glanced around, no one even bothered to look up to see why Rajeev was shouting. She lamented to herself, "Seems like a daily shouting routine for everyone... I am so dead. A bad start to the rest of my so-called corporate life."

The day ended with nearly twenty abuses hurled at her regarding her incompetence and dumbness by Rajeev.

Nikita couldn't wait to run into Rahul's arms. "I missed you the most," Nikita mumbled as she hugged Rahul in the car parking lot. Rahul was confused. He had just made her eat his specialty pancakes that morning, and not even a few hours had passed before he came back to pick her up. Yet, the happy Nikita from earlier now had a sullen face.

"Are you okay? I think the job is affecting your mind! I told you not to do this. People are dying for you to become an actress, and you want to be a clerk moving around files," Rahul shouted at Nikita. Nikita shouted back, "Enough of everyone bossing me around. I have heard enough shouting today from Mr. Arrogant. I am not taking it anymore, especially from my best friend."

Before Rahul could ask who Mr. Arrogant was, Nikita asked him to drive far, far away from the office, as she didn't want to see the place any more than necessary to get her monthly salary. They reached her apartment in one of the posh areas of Lower Parel, which she shared with her roommate Priya. Rahul received another hug from Priya, and his face got plastered with kisses. Yes, Nikita's roommate is also Rahul's girlfriend, a fact that Nikita hated but couldn't figure out why. She just turned her face away.

TWO
CRUSHING HARD

"Rahul! You need to drop me. I'm late again. Mr. Arrogant is going to kill me." Nikita rushed to the office, hoping against hope that Rajeev wouldn't notice her late entrance. But, as usual, he was waiting at her desk. To add insult to injury, he spent the next hour loudly lecturing her about the value of time and another hour criticizing the report she had submitted yesterday.

Feeling dejected, Nikita sat down, and her cubicle mate Sahil tried to console her, pointing out that since Rajeev hadn't had a chance to scold anyone yet, she was his first target. Everyone in the office was nice and helpful to her, even the senior managers, but Nikita couldn't understand why she was so desperate for Mr. Arrogant's approval.

It had been a week, and she had already heard a hundred times that her work was not up to the mark and that she was a disgrace as an intern. Her favorite place had become the washroom, where she found peace and quiet to cry her heart out, as there weren't many girls on her team or the entire floor who could listen to her rant.

As she came out of the washroom, having finished her crying session, Sahil asked her if she wanted coffee. "You don't need to cheer me up; it's my daily routine. I think Mr. Arrogant can't have lunch unless he scolds me first." This made Sahil laugh out loud, but it also made someone else turn in anger. Rajeev's cabin was quite near the coffee machine area where most of the staff gathered to gossip, making it pretty audible to him as well. He had designed it that way. He liked to analyze the people he worked with and be aware of everything happening around him because the one thing he hated was surprises.

"Did that newbie MBA graduate call me arrogant? I'm going to make sure she gets so many assignments that her brain finally learns something her college failed to teach!" Rajeev fumed as he overheard their conversation.

Meanwhile, Sahil was consoling Nikita, saying, "The guy is frustrated and a womanizer. You need to complain to HR soon so he learns how to speak to women." Nikita retorted, "I don't want to play the woman card, and why should he talk to me differently compared to you all? I am his employee, and if I am doing something wrong, how else will I learn? I'm actually happy that he doesn't treat me like I'm some fragile doll who will break if he scolds me. He treats me as an equal, and I like that."

Sahil was shocked. "You girls are weird. All of you like psychotic guys only. When will we good guys be liked?" Nikita playfully banged her file on his head and said, "Take me for a Starbucks coffee next time, then I'll give you an answer." Sahil shrugged and said, "That's why I'll never get dates. I'm a poor man."

Rajeev was even more shocked than Sahil. Why did she defend me? Sahil is right. She could easily have made an issue out of it. After a long time, he smiled, thinking, "So, she likes me, huh?" He called her inside, but to his surprise, he couldn't find the words he wanted to say. He tried to think of a plausible work excuse but blurted out, "What are you doing at 7?"

Nikita, nervously staring at her floaters and regretting not wearing formal shoes, looked up in surprise at this unexpected question. "I had promised to treat Sahil to Starbucks coffee, but if there's work, I can stay back." Rajeev felt his smile vanish, replaced by a rage he struggled to control. He managed to blurt out, "Yes, there is work."

Nikita waited for a moment, but Rajeev, with his red eyes fixed on her, said nothing more. She excused herself, saying, "Sure, sir, let me know." As soon as she was out the door, Rajeev punched his desk and muttered under his breath, "I will make sure that dumbass never drinks coffee again."

"Come on, let's go. Tell him you'll finish this tomorrow," Sahil nagged, showing Nikita the clock every five minutes. Rajeev had been watching for half an hour and finally couldn't take it any longer. "Nikita, can you please check the reports you sent me using your brain and eyes?" he shouted, startling Sahil more than Nikita. "Just come with your laptop. Everything needs to be taught from scratch. What were you doing in college?" Nikita shot an apologetic look at a dejected Sahil before rushing inside, signaling him to leave without her.

After nearly an hour of correcting reports and constantly glancing at her, Rajeev finally broke the silence. "Hey, I'm not a coffee fan, but I guess I owe you a Starbucks coffee since I made you work overtime. Just come; it'll make me feel less guilty," he said.

Nikita reluctantly agreed but suggested a café she was familiar with instead. After a few moments of awkward silence and staring at her coffee, Nikita got her second surprise of the day when Rajeev casually asked, "So, are you dating Sahil?"

"What? No. I mean, I've only known him for a week. What made you think that?" Nikita was puzzled by his sudden interest in her dating life. More worrying was her next answer: "I don't have a boyfriend." "Oh my god, why did I say this? He didn't even ask that question, and I'm blurting out irrelevant information. No wonder he thinks I'm an idiot," Nikita thought, wishing for an earthquake to swallow the coffee shop and save her from this embarrassing situation. If only she could see the smile that her statement had brought to Rajeev's face.

Rajeev insisted on dropping Nikita at her home. His curiosity piqued when he saw her lavish apartment. "Why are you working as an intern if you can afford such a place?" he couldn't help but ask.

"This isn't my flat," Nikita replied. "My friend Rahul rented it to me at a nominal rate because he wants all his friends to live in the same building. He's a bit eccentric. I'll introduce you to him someday. Thanks a lot for the coffee, Mr. ... Sir," she caught herself just in time from calling him Mr. Arrogant, then quickly ran into her apartment.

"Why is Mr. Arrogant dropping you off? I thought you two hated each other," Rahul said, trailing behind Nikita, increasingly irritated by her repeated "I don't know" responses to all his queries. Rahul's curiosity was matched only by Rajeev's, who was determined to understand the connection between Nikita and Rahul's apartment.

Rajeev gave clear instructions to Philip, his trusted aide since childhood: "I want to know everything about her—school, college, present life. Her friends, enemies—the entire family tree. I need it all." Philip, a reliable go-getter, always executed tasks without question. Rajeev trusted him implicitly, especially now, as he found himself deeply infatuated with a girl he barely knew.

"This is bad. I can't be this clueless. I need all the information before I make any decisions," Rajeev muttered to himself, trying to rationalize his actions. Little did he know, he had already fallen for her, and his life was about to change forever.

THREE

THE FIRST STEP

Nikita had been at the job for just six months when she received her confirmation. With it came her first gift from Mr. Arrogant himself, Rajeev. "We're going to Coimbatore tomorrow," he announced. "We need to visit the company to understand the processes better. You need to come along and get firsthand knowledge of what you're actually working on when you make excel spreadsheets."

Rajeev had just invited her on her first official trip, even though it was only for a weekend. Sahil, however, was not pleased and tried to dampen Nikita's spirits. "How will you survive two days alone with that guy? He'll insult you endlessly. Tell HR you can't go alone with him because you don't feel safe," Sahil urged, trying to convince her by the coffee machine, while Rajeev listened from his cabin.

"I wish I could fire this dumbass. What's his problem?" Rajeev fumed, mentally conjuring up a string of insults for Sahil. But Nikita's voice snapped him back to reality. "Have you lost it, Sahil? Why would I complain to anyone? I feel absolutely safe with Rajeev. I don't even think he's noticed I'm a girl; he's too busy shouting at me to make sure I learn the work. I knew nothing about this industry or this job, and he's taught me everything from scratch. None of the other interns have had the chance to work on such a major consulting project in just six months. I'm so lucky to have him as my manager."

Rajeev felt a surge of pride listening to Nikita defend him, but then he blushed as she added, "Plus, he's so cute when he shouts. I just keep staring at him and don't even hear the insults he's throwing at me." Sahil was shocked. "Have you fallen in love with this abusive guy? God help you!"

Nikita brushed him off, "I don't know, but I like Mr. Arrogant." Rajeev, trying to suppress a smile even though no one could see him in his cabin, thought, "So that's your nickname for me... Miss... hmm... what should I call you? I can only think of cartoons. Yes, you're my Miss Cartoon."

Rajeev came out of his cabin, glaring at Sahil, and asked Nikita to meet him in the parking lot. Nikita quickly grabbed her bag and called Rahul to inform him of her plans.

"Why do you have to go out at night with random people you don't even like? I just don't understand these 9-to-5 jobs and being a slave to a boss you have to pretend to like just so they pay your salary," Rahul vented. He hated her career choice and always encouraged her to join him and Priya in the movie industry, but Nikita felt she wasn't cut out for it. Dieting daily, exercising constantly, and wearing loads of makeup every day would kill her.

She remembered those days in school when she did a few short acting stints with Rahul and Priya to earn extra money for her college fees. She would always be indebted to them for that, but consulting was her dream. She hoped against hope that Rahul would understand and stop irritating her about it every day.

Rajeev knew her entire background from Philip. He knew how she had put herself through college by working in a few music videos and movies with her school friend, Rahul. Rahul had not only helped her get these roles but also provided the flat where she now lived with Priya.

Despite her connections in the acting world, Nikita wanted to pursue an MBA, and Rahul had supported her in every way possible, including dropping her off at college and company interviews. The exact nature of Rahul and Nikita's relationship was still unclear to Rajeev, but Philip had not given up on finding answers.

Rajeev snapped out of his thoughts as Nikita entered his car. "We'll drive to the airport. In the meantime, you can brief me on what you've understood about this project so far."

The drive to the airport, the flight, and the subsequent drive to the hotel were remarkably free of any displays of anger from Mr. Arrogant. Instead, Rajeev was unexpectedly helpful, patiently answering even the silliest of her doubts. Nikita felt skeptical, suspecting this was merely the calm before the storm. Little did she know, it was new for Rajeev too.

Rajeev was surprised by the amount of effort he was putting into not shouting. He didn't understand why it had suddenly become so important to him not to upset her or make that cute smile vanish from her face.

The hotel manager had given them adjoining rooms with a connecting door, making it easy for Rajeev to barge in barely two minutes after they had parted ways. "I'm sorry, I didn't realize this was a connecting door. Get ready and come to my room so we can plan for the meeting tomorrow," he said.

Even as he spoke, he was thinking, "What is wrong with me? Why can't I stay away from her for even a few minutes? What a stupid excuse I had to make when all we did on the way was talk about the project. What if she understands my ulterior motive and doesn't come?" Before he could finish his thoughts, Nikita was standing there with her laptop and notebook.

He made her sit with him on the bed, and they resumed their discussion, but all he could focus on was her face. When her hair fell across her face, blocking his view, Rajeev instinctively reached out to tuck it back, which made Nikita uncomfortable. She stopped talking, but Rajeev, having made his first move, wasn't about to stop. He leaned in for their first kiss, half-expecting to hear a "What are you doing?" But, as usual, Nikita surprised him.

"I have never done this, so I may be bad at it. Please don't mind or get put off or something, because I really like you," she said. He pulled back, staring at her in surprise. "What? You haven't kissed anyone? You're almost 26," he blurted out, remembering the details from the bio-data Philip had collected about her.

Nikita was scared. "Why are you angry? I'm sorry. I just didn't want to start something on a false note." Rajeev had an incredulous look on his face, thinking, "Is this girl for real? Is she that innocent? Why is she telling me all this? But why did I stop? No, no, no... I can't be falling for her. I hate these emotional attachments."

Before he could say anything, Nikita rushed to hug him, mumbling apologies. He came back to his senses and cupped her face in his hands. "Why are you sorry? I just want us to take it slow if you've waited this long. If this is your first time, you need to be sure about me. I have to fly to Goa for another client. You should go back, and we'll start with a proper date when I return in two days." He kissed her forehead, walked her to her room, and put her to bed.

Nikita was too excited to sleep and needed to talk to her best friend. She messaged Rahul since it was too late to call: "I kissed Mr. Arrogant... I think I am in love. Will tell you the full story when I return." Little did she know, neither Rajeev nor Rahul could sleep that night.

Rahul read the message as Priya slept in his arms. He couldn't call Nikita back and didn't want to because he was seething with rage. Rajeev, on the other hand, was still trying to decode Nikita. Unable to sleep, he decided to reach out to Philip again. "You need to find out everything about her personal relationships, preferably with photographs. Follow her for a day and gauge her routine. I need every detail about how she spends her time."

All three of them spent a sleepless night, unaware that things would only get worse from here.

FOUR
THE BIG FIGHT

Nikita and Rahul had been having continuous fights for two days since she returned from her trip. "I don't get it. How could you get so close to your own boss? Do you have any self-respect? Do you want your entire office to gossip about you?" Rahul shouted, following her around the apartment. Nikita tried to avoid him by covering her ears.

Priya, calmly sitting on the sofa, interjected, "Maybe he really likes her. What's the big deal? They're both single and adults." Nikita stopped moving, feeling a surge of confidence from Priya's support. She turned to Rahul and shouted, "My life, my wish. I like him. Let people talk about whatever they want."

Rahul's incessant nagging hadn't stopped since Nikita's return. He constantly told her how foolish she was to be used by her boss. While they waited in line for coffee, Rahul couldn't stop talking. "Is this the image you want to portray? Do you think that guy fell in love with you in six months without even going on a date? All you've done together is work. Guys just want one thing from girls. Why don't you understand such a simple thing? Get out of your romantic world, Nikki. Not everyone is a romantic like you."

Nikita was getting frustrated with Rahul's overprotectiveness. "I've never had a boyfriend because of these stupid ideas you've pushed into my mind. Rajeev is different, and to prove it, I'm taking him on a date tonight. He's coming back today, and we'll go on a normal date—only talking." Rahul, still frustrated, didn't give up on his lecture until he dropped her off at the office.

Rajeev saw Rahul hug Nikita through his window but couldn't hear that Rahul was warning her to be careful of Rajeev, not wanting to see her hurt. Rajeev noticed the blush on Nikita's face, unaware that she was imagining how she would ask him out on a date. His eyes filled with anger as he looked again at the photographs Philip had given him upon his arrival in Mumbai. They were full of images of Rahul and Nikita hugging in a café. The worst one showed Rahul kissing Nikita on the cheek, which Rajeev tore up in a fit of rage. His anger didn't subside even as Nikita entered his cabin.

"Haven't you learned to knock yet? Just when I think you can't get any dumber, you prove me wrong. What is so urgent now?" Rajeev snapped. Nikita was shocked by his sudden change in attitude. She thought maybe this was how he would always behave in the office to keep things professional, so she went ahead with her plan of asking him out.

"I was wondering if you would like to go on a dinner date with me today," she asked, but she was unprepared for his curt reply. Rajeev looked up in surprise and asked, "Why?"

Her mind kept replaying Rahul's words about how Rajeev would never go on a date, but she still refused to believe it. Smiling sheepishly and blushing, Nikita tried again. "I thought we should get to know each other better so that what happened at the hotel wouldn't be awkward next time."

This time she had Rajeev's complete attention, but his words brought her world crashing down. "Why do we need a date for that? You can tell me your requirement so that the next transaction will be smoother. Also, I hope you're not expecting a promotion for just one night or even a salary increment. I like to keep professional and personal life separate. Just tell me your number, and the money will be transferred to your account next time we decide to do it. Now please leave and let me do my work. This is neither the place nor the time to discuss these things."

Nikita was too shocked to say a word. She moved out of Rajeev's office with tears streaming down her face. She couldn't see the tears in Rajeev's eyes either, only the anger he directed at her. "A barely out-of-college girl cannot make a fool out of me," he muttered, tearing up the photographs and flushing them down the toilet.

Nikita, in the bathroom, desperately dialed Rahul's number. "You were right, you were right," was all Rahul could make out between her incessant sobs. He told her he would be at her office in an hour and rushed out of the shoot, leaving Priya staring after him. Priya couldn't understand his obsessive behavior towards Nikita over the past three days, but for now, she could do nothing. She swore to change this situation soon.

Rajeev was still fuming as he looked out of his window and saw Nikita get into Rahul's car. Unable to tolerate it any longer, he rushed out, only to be stopped by Sahil.

"Sir, Nikita wasn't feeling well, so she had to leave urgently. She transferred all her files and spoke with HR too. Let me know if you need me to work on any details," Sahil blabbered. Rajeev barely listened; his thoughts consumed with anger. "It's better this way," he thought. "If

I had to see that conniving girl's face any longer, I would have lost my mind."

Priya watched as Rahul consoled Nikita, who finally fell asleep after crying for an hour. "I will kill that guy," Rahul fumed, but before he could say anything else, Priya's question left him dumbstruck. "Why do you care? Isn't this what you were telling her would happen? You should be happy that you were correct. Why are you getting so affected?"

Rahul was confused and angry. "Are you serious? What kind of friend are you, not getting affected by her crying?" he shouted at Priya and started to head back to Nikita's room. Priya's next comment stopped him in his tracks. "Maybe you should think about what kind of friend you are if this is affecting you so much."

FIVE

THE JEALOUSY BUG BITES EVERYONE

It had been two days since Nikita had gone to the office or left her bedroom. "Dude, you and your room are stinking, and you wonder why that boss of yours didn't want to date you!" Priya joked as Rahul opened the curtains in Nikita's room. This brought on another outburst of crying from Nikita, and Rahul rushed to her side.

"Priya, just leave for now. Go to my flat. I'll come there," Rahul said, trying to console Nikita. Priya attempted to approach Nikita, saying she was just joking, but Rahul firmly sent her away. As Priya left for Rahul's flat, which was right opposite theirs, the last thing she saw was Rahul cupping Nikita's face, trying to cheer her up.

"Let's go out. Do you want to go to your favorite café? I know coffee always cheers you up," Rahul kept trying to distract her, but the humiliation from that day at the office was still fresh in her mind.

"How will I face him or anyone in the office? I think I got so desperate for love since I never had a boyfriend. I admire the open relationship that you and Priya have. No emotional expectations or attachments. You can be with whoever you want and still care for each other. I think I need to become like that and have zero expectations. I'm too old-fashioned, looking for matrimonial-type dating while the world has moved on to casual dating. Maybe I should try some of those dating apps; that should cheer me up." Rahul's heart skipped a beat, and the anxiety he felt when she wanted to date Rajeev came rushing back.

"You just need a break from guys. Men just want one thing, and you're not ready for that, so focus on your career for now. Try to find a new job away from that crackhead boss of yours so you can be happier." Rahul tried to steer her away from the dating app conversation, suddenly feeling insecure. He couldn't imagine Nikita on a date with anyone else, so he aimed to push these thoughts out of her mind too. "Whatever you want to do on a date—big restaurants, fancy shopping, movies, dancing—you can do with me. That's what best friends are for. So, try to find a new job and forget about relationships for now. At least come to the party tonight. It'll cheer you up."

Nikita got up, determination in her eyes. "You're right. I need a new job and more money. My career is my only goal. I don't want coffee or parties until I find myself a new job. You and Priya should go; I'll be busy updating my resume. You're always right. What would I do without you, Rahul?" She hugged him.

Rahul stroked her back and whispered in her ear, "You will never be without me. It's extremely difficult to get rid of me." They both laughed, but their moment of levity enraged Priya, who had just returned to the apartment and was silently watching them from the door.

Priya and Rahul were fighting as they left for the party. "I fail to understand this extra concern you suddenly have for Nikita," Priya said. Rahul retorted, "And I fail to understand your indifference to your own roommate and probably the only friend you have." This infuriated Priya further. "Are you trying to tell me I have no friends? You're going to a party hosted by my friend."

Rahul didn't want to get into it, still worried about Nikita at home. "Yes, another one of your boyfriends. Anyways Priya, I don't care. We decided to have an open relationship to avoid such conversations. Let's not get into what I'm feeling about whom. Let's stick to the pact we made. Now smile as we arrive at the party hosted by one of your many 'friends'."

They mingled with others at the party but couldn't shake off their uneasy feelings. Neither noticed Philip discreetly taking their photographs from a short distance away.

SIX

REALIZATION OF THE MISTAKE

Nikita returned after five days, prepared to offer an explanation to Mr. Arrogant about her sudden absence, but the only person who welcomed her was Sahil. "I missed you, man. Please don't disappear like this again. Your Mr. Arrogant made my life hell in your absence. I don't want to take your place ever," Sahil complained as he hugged her. "Who is in his cabin? I want to explain my five-day absence to him as soon as I can and get it over with," Nikita said, attempting to peer through the translucent glass doors.

"It's his personal assistant, or valet, or butler, or something. I'm not sure, but he's like his right-hand man and handles all his personal tasks. We've seen him around sometimes when the boss doesn't go home. This time, he hasn't gone home for the last five days. He's been working non-stop and driving us crazy in the process. You went AWOL at the right time and escaped his psychotic behavior," Sahil explained as they both sat down, and Nikita began to gather project updates from him.

It was going to be a long wait for Nikita. Inside his cabin, Rajeev paced the floor, frustration radiating from him as he shouted at Philip. "I don't understand your investigation! First, you give me photographs of Nikita and Rahul, and now you're telling me he has such photos with every girl? Why did you come to me with a half-baked report?"

Philip was already feeling deeply apologetic. He prided himself on understanding people, yet he had clearly misjudged Rahul. "I'm sorry, Rajeev. I should have done a more thorough job. It seems Rahul is friendly with every girl he knows, meets, or talks to even for a few minutes. I was focusing on Nikita's background at the time and failed to follow up on Rahul. From what I've gathered, Rahul is in an 'open relationship'—a term youngsters use nowadays—with Priya, who is Nikita's roommate. I need more time to fully understand Rahul's character."

Rajeev's frustration only grew with the explanation. "Come back when you have the full story," he snapped. As Philip left, Rajeev noticed Nikita sitting outside. For a moment, their eyes met before she quickly looked away as the door closed behind Philip.

Rajeev was unsure what to say to her, still scrambling for an excuse to make things right. Before he could figure out how to apologize, Nikita entered.

"I'm sorry, I forgot to knock," she said quickly, then stepped outside again, giving Rajeev a moment to regain his composure. He wanted to apologize profusely, but his words failed him as Nikita began speaking. "I skipped the last five days because it was too awkward for me to face you after the way I behaved. I had a sort of crush on you, and my romantic brain started imagining a dramatic boyfriend-girlfriend relationship, which was totally inappropriate considering you're my manager. I'm looking for opportunities outside and have already submitted my resignation to HR this morning. Since I just got confirmed, I need to serve a notice period of two months, so you'll have to endure me a little longer. I'll explain all my work to Sahil to ensure a smooth transfer of responsibilities. I'm sorry again for my behavior and will try to stay out of your way until my notice period is up."

Before Rajeev could process the blow, Nikita left the room. He felt as if the air had been knocked out of him and sank into his chair, exasperated. "Why didn't I apologize? Why didn't I explain my situation? No, no, no. She can't resign. How could she even think of leaving me?" His initial weakness turned to anger. He was astonished by how strongly she affected him and couldn't understand her control over him. He knew he couldn't let her go without a fight.

His anger at being affected by Nikita was palpable. Rahul had arrived at her office to pick her up, but the workload Rajeev had assigned to Nikita was endless, forcing her to request a leave. Nikita was nervous about entering the cabin again, but with Rahul's music album launch party approaching, she had no choice. She gathered her courage and timidly asked, "Can I finish the work tomorrow? I have an urgent personal issue to attend to."

Rajeev had seen Rahul's car pull up, which only fueled his already simmering anger. "If you want to leave with your boyfriend in his fancy car rather than complete the work you're paid to do, that's your choice. After all, you've already resigned," he snapped.

Unable to stop himself from making the snide remark, Rajeev watched meekly as Nikita retorted angrily, "Rahul is not my boyfriend. He's just here to pick me up. It's already getting late, and since I've resigned, I don't think I'm doing any injustice to my salary. In any case, you can dock my pay for today if it makes you feel better."

Nikita walked off, leaving Rajeev alone with his thoughts. Instead of feeling angry about her outburst, he found himself smiling at the words "not my boyfriend." For once, Philip was right.

It was Rahul's album launch, with Priya as the main lead in the music videos. Rahul was busy consoling the despondent Nikita yet again. Priya had seen Rahul being friendly with many girls, a pattern that typically lasted a week or two, but this felt different. They had been friends since school, and Rahul had always been protective of Nikita, but this time, his behavior seemed more intense.

Priya noticed a possessive, jealous side of Rahul—a side she hadn't seen since they started dating in school. Watching Rahul behave this way toward someone else stirred feelings of jealousy in her.She had understood their feelings for each other before they had even realized it themselves, and she didn't like it. Priya knew she needed to act before Rahul and Nikita fully grasped their feelings for one another.

Rahul wanted to be happy that Nikita was leaving her current job, as he always wished she would work with him instead of such corporate roles. However, seeing her upset over another guy troubled him deeply. Why was she so affected by a random man? It had been six days already, and he was still trying to comfort her, but her tears were for someone else. This only fueled his anger even more.

"This two-day relationship has taken such a toll on her that she doesn't even want to celebrate my big moment with me today," he thought bitterly. "I need to find a new job for her so she can leave this place sooner. I won't allow her boss anywhere near her. This has to end."

It was almost midnight when they finally reached home after the party. After Nikita fell asleep, Rahul left her side and lay down next to Priya. They both stared ahead, silently planning their next moves. They knew they needed to win this battle of love at any cost.

SEVEN

START OF A FRIENDSHIP

Rahul gently pulled Nikita out of bed and handed her a cup of coffee. "Can you at least glance at your job interview emails and start some preparation instead of wasting all your time in bed?" he asked.

Nikita reluctantly looked at the laptop screen, blinking in surprise as she saw at least seven interview invites. "How did you do it? I didn't even apply to them!" she exclaimed, hugging Rahul so suddenly that they both tumbled onto the bed.

"Wow, this is a really romantic moment, but I wish you had at least brushed your teeth," Rahul joked, only to be playfully punched by her. "Get dressed," he continued. "Your first interview is scheduled for this evening, so you better start preparing. I want you to get over this Rajeev chapter forever."

Nikita was just entering the office building when she saw Rajeev getting out of a car and kissing a girl who had driven him to work. As the car swept by, she tried to peek inside, feeling she had found the answer to her unasked question of why Rajeev was never interested in her.

Rajeev approached the elevator, and Nikita decided to make small talk. "Your girlfriend is really beautiful. I'm sorry about that day. I didn't know you were in a relationship, or I would have stayed miles away. I'm trying to erase that day from my mind. I wish I could erase it from yours too."

As the elevator doors opened, Nikita rushed out, saying "Sorry" again, but Rajeev was lost in his thoughts. He wanted to tell her that the girl she saw wasn't his girlfriend but stopped himself. He didn't want to appear vulnerable in front of Nikita again, though he was still angry about her resignation. "Why don't I want her to leave?" he wondered. "I went on a date last night with that girl to forget about Nikita, but I ended up thinking about Nikita the whole time. This has got to stop!"

Rajeev wanted to clear the confusion between them, but he was unable to find the time to talk to her. He kept getting refused whenever he asked for time alone with her to bring up the subject. When he finally mustered the courage to ask her out for coffee, he was immediately turned down. Nikita tried to refuse politely, citing a job interview, but her repeated rejections were wearing on his nerves. He hated losing, and the thought of not seeing her after two months was unbearable.

He knew he had to make a move before he made the situation worse by hiding his true feelings, so he said, "You don't have to quit because of me. We can start fresh. Hi, I'm Rajeev. Do you want to be friends?"

Nikita stopped him mid-sentence. "I'm quitting because of me. I have a huge crush on you, and I can only get over it by leaving. Seeing your girlfriend in the car today made me realize why you didn't take me seriously that day. It's okay,

I'm not mad, but I really need to get over my feelings for you. No hard feelings!"

"This girl always leaves me speechless. How innocently she can express her feelings! Why am I so scared of speaking the truth?" Rajeev wondered, smiling to himself. His smile quickly faded when he looked out and saw Nikita being picked up by Rahul once again in the car parking lot.

Jealousy and anger flared up once more. "I need to understand this Rahul chapter of her life before I can even begin to understand my own feelings," he thought. Determined, he picked up the phone and called Philip again.

EIGHT

IS THIS LOVE?

"I got the offer! I got the job!" Nikita burst into Rahul's apartment, jumping up and down with excitement. "Finally! I got an offer! Thank you, Rahul!" Priya, watching from the kitchen, couldn't help but intervene in this overenthusiastic celebration. "It was your skills that landed you the job. Rahul, or anyone else, doesn't deserve the credit!"

Nikita refused to listen. "No way. For two months, this guy has been finding job notifications, interviews, employment ads, and taking me to every interview. I think he wanted me to get a new job more than I did. What would I do without you, Rahul? Why aren't all guys as sweet as you?" Priya understood Nikita's feelings and had also witnessed a changed Rahul over the past two months. His closeness with Nikita was making her even more uneasy.

Nikita looked chirpier than usual today, while Rajeev grew gloomier and angrier as her last day approached. Whenever he considered apologizing for his behavior, he stopped himself, seeing her happiness about leaving the office—and especially him—growing by the moment.

"Why is she so happy about not seeing me again? What happened to her talks about liking me? She is such a...

LIAR!" he fumed internally. This thought only intensified his anger at himself, as her resignation seemed to be affecting him more than it was affecting her. Unable to contain his frustration, he lashed out with sarcasm, wanting her to feel the same pain he was experiencing. "You seem quite happy about quitting. Is it because you'll get to spend more time with your boyfriend Rahul, or has he found some work for you in one of the third-rate music videos he creates?"

Nikita was taken aback, surprised that Rajeev knew about this part of her past. "He's not my boyfriend, and his videos are not third-rate. I worked in those videos to pay my college fees. Rahul's videos get a lot of views; he has a huge team that works on the creation and promotion. Anyway, I'll be out of your hair in a few days, so you won't have to endure me any longer."

As Nikita walked away, Rajeev cursed himself for making matters worse yet again. He knew about her past thanks to Philip, but he couldn't resist hurling insults at her. Why couldn't he control his emotions around her? He realized he needed to make peace and try again before it was too late.

As evening approached and Nikita's departure drew near, Rajeev decided to make one last attempt at asking her out. He meticulously calculated the timing of the elevator, her movements, and his driving, aiming to drive past her just as she left the office building.

"Hey, do you want a lift?" he called out, pulling up beside her. "Actually, I wanted to visit that café near your house you mentioned to Sahil. I was wondering if you could show me the way." Trying to sound casual, Rajeev looked at her with the most innocent face he could muster.

Nikita was surprised by the offer but wanted things to normalize before she left the company. Also, her Uber was running late, so she decided to take him up on the offer. "Sure, why not," she said, getting into the car.

"This is the place. You can drop me here; my flat is just a walkable distance away. Don't forget to try the frappe. I know you have black coffee every day at the office, but this frappe is special," Nikita said, preparing to walk away.

Just as she turned, she felt Rajeev's hand gently pulling her back. She was surprised by his sudden friendliness, especially after he had yelled at her for some report an hour ago, criticizing her comprehension skills. "I hate sitting alone in a restaurant. I'd appreciate your company for half an hour," Rajeev said, his smile genuinely charming. Nikita was reminded why she had a crush on him in the first place.

He ordered a black coffee for himself and a frappe for her. "You never change your routine. Why do you hate trying new things? A spoonful of extra sugar won't kill you!" Nikita teased, knowing that soon he would no longer be her manager. Rajeev grumbled, "I hate changes in my daily routine," and stared at her, leaving it up to her to continue the conversation or let the awkward silence linger.

"So, why are you trying a new café in a completely out-of-your-way area?" Nikita asked, still failing to understand Rajeev. As always, he refused to explain and instead surprised her with a personal question. "So, you and Rahul live together? He seems to be your personal chauffeur, driving you to the office almost every day."

Nikita couldn't comprehend his sudden interest in Rahul. "Are you a fan of his or something? You ask about him a lot. He's my best friend and gets a little overprotective about me, but he goes overboard for all his friends. He's just a great guy. If you're a fan, I can introduce you. He's quite down-to-earth and very enthusiastic about meeting his fans."

Now it was Rajeev's turn to misunderstand the situation. "I'm not a fan, but you seem to be a huge admirer of Rahul. So why aren't you dating him? I've never heard you sing praises for anyone like you do for him."

Nikita laughed. "I wish! But he has a girlfriend—who happens to be my roommate. I had a huge crush on him in school, but he's been with Priya since then. I think they recently celebrated their ten-year anniversary or something. Anyway, I'm not his type. He's quite a popular rock star, and with his recent entry into movies, his female fan following has been increasing day by day. He has a lot of girls fawning over him. So, I'm happy just being his friend."

Rajeev was taken aback by her honest confession, thinking, "This girl just speaks her mind without any care." He said, "Rahul is making a fool out of you and your roommate. His cozy pictures with a lot of so-called fans and peers are all over the media these days."

Rajeev's obsession with Rahul was starting to irk her. "I didn't know you paid attention to any kind of entertainment media news. You used to think all news channels were getting dumber day by day. Anyway, you've misunderstood him. Rahul is not dating any of those girls. He just goes out once or twice because he and Priya have an open relationship. He's not fooling anyone, as he tells them about Priya upfront. The media just likes making gossip out of thin air," Nikita said, getting up to leave.

Rajeev, desperate to spend more time with her, grabbed her hand. He realized too late that his sarcasm had hurt her again. "I was just trying to understand you and your relationship with Rahul. You seem to like him so much that you're fighting with me over a few words I said against him.

What were you doing with me in that hotel then?" Rajeev tried to open up about his feelings, but Nikita's answer put a stop to his train of thought.

"Rahul is the nicest guy I know and treats me like family. Anyone I've tried to date has either used me to get Priya's number or just wanted a casual date to be around Priya. I know I'm not pretty, and being friends with an attractive girl like Priya has only made things worse. I do have a liking for Rahul, but I know he and Priya are a forever kind of thing, and I don't want to get in the middle of that."

Rajeev's fears and assumptions were correct, but being right didn't save him from the heartbreak he felt at that moment. "So, you're saying you actually love Rahul but can't do much about it because he's in love with someone else?"

It was Nikita's turn to be at a loss for words, so she kept sipping her frappe. Finally, she got up, frustrated, and shouted, "Yes, I guess," before running out of the café, leaving Rajeev staring ahead with tears welling up in his eyes.

NINE

MISSION-RAHUL

After several sleepless nights, struggling with her feelings for Rahul, Nikita finally had a happy day: it was her last day at the office. She could finally put her professional problems aside and start thinking about how to solve her newfound personal problem—Rahul. Rahul offered to drop her off at the office. "So, finally you don't have to see that Mr. Arrogant's face again," he said.

Nikita had been trying to keep her distance from Rahul since the day she met Rajeev at the café, so she meekly replied, "Rahul, I don't want to bother you. Also, I think you hate that guy more than I do. I have no idea why. If you see him there, you might create a scene."

"That guy was a douche, as I rightly predicted, but you refused to listen to me. I don't hate him; I just know these types of guys and their intentions. I've told you multiple times to stay away from such people, but if only you would listen," Rahul retorted.

Just then, the cab arrived. Nikita decided to leave but delivered a parting shot to Rahul. "You have a problem with any guy I try to date. I think you're the reason I still haven't had a single boyfriend. Rajeev was not a douche. He told me upfront what he expected and never forced me to do anything. We just wanted different things from a relationship. I still like him for his honest and candid behavior." Nikita couldn't see the jealousy and anger in Rahul's eyes as she rushed out to the cab.

Rajeev was despondent, wondering if he would ever see Nikita again. He pretended not to care, hiding in his cabin all day. His heart leaped with joy when Nikita entered, as usual without knocking. Little did he know that his happiness was about to grow further as Nikita would solve his problem of staying in touch with her even after she quits.

"It's my last day, and I wanted to ask a favor. Can we meet after hours for a coffee?" Nikita asked. Nikita inviting him seemed like a hint to Rajeev that he still had some time to think of a plan to keep her in his life. "Maybe she wants to stay in touch too, and that's the favor she wants. But why is she quitting the job because of me? No, I need to come up with something. Maybe an outside project or a training... think, think, Rajeev!"

With these thoughts swirling in his mind, Rajeev racked his brain until it was time to leave for the coffee date. He completely forgot about his work and appointments for the day. "This girl is going to get me fired one day!" he smiled, as he prepped the speech, he planned to give Nikita to convince her to stay in touch with him.

As Rajeev was gathering the courage to talk, he nearly choked on his coffee when Nikita spoke, "I need a favor from you. Teach me how to make Rahul fall in love with me. You were the one who made me realize I love Rahul, so you need to help me. I don't have any other friends—basically, all my friends are Rahul's friends. Plus, I see all these hot girls fawning over you when you're not exactly Tom Cruise, so give me tips on how to make people like me. I don't have anything else to offer you in return, other than that I'll owe you one. So, what do you think?"

Rajeev was astonished at how Nikita always managed to shock and hurt him with her heartfelt confessions. He managed to say, "Let's say I waste my time and energy teaching something that can't be taught. Are you even sure you love him? Not so long ago, you were saying you loved me. Why don't you concentrate on your new job instead? I can actually give you helpful tips for that instead of wasting time on your personal issues."

Nikita was not ready to give up easily. "You've always given me professional tips, and I'm sure you'll keep helping me in that department forever. But I need help in this personal life department too. Please, you're the only one I trust with all this. I don't have any other friends."

Her blind trust in him helped heal the hurt caused by her obsession with Rahul, so Rajeev agreed to help her. They spent the rest of the evening planning when and where they could meet to discuss "Mission Rahul." Rajeev couldn't believe that he had spent two hours talking about Nikita's new job and her feelings for Rahul. Normally, he wouldn't waste even an extra minute in his meetings on topics outside the agenda. She was making him lose control, and he hated that. He resolved to regain control of his life and not let anyone have such an influence over him.

However, this resolve was broken the same night when Nikita called him to discuss how Rahul and Priya were irritating her. Rajeev listened for an hour until Nikita fell asleep. Shaking his head as he cut the call, he realized he had lost this game and, more importantly, himself to Nikita for good.

TEN

RAHUL GETS JEALOUS, AGAIN!

"Just a minute," Nikita said for the tenth time as she left the movie to take a call. She had been busier lately after starting her new job. "What's so important at night that movies and sleep have taken a back seat? It's just been a week at your new job, and you've already made quite a few close friends," Rahul inquired sarcastically, trying to hide his growing jealousy as he pulled Nikita into his arms.

"It's a colleague, some work-related queries. Not important," Nikita replied, trying to get out of his embrace as she noticed Priya glaring at her. Rahul had become extra curious and a bit jealous lately. Her "Mission Rahul," which she was planning with Rajeev, seemed to be working; so much so that even Priya noticed the change in Rahul's behavior, and she did not look very pleased.

As the movie ended, Priya and Rahul got up to head to Rahul's apartment, while Nikita stepped out to attend Rajeev's call, oblivious to Rahul's eyes watching her every move. "I think I left my phone behind. You go ahead and sleep, I'll be back in a minute," Rahul told Priya, leaving her in their flat and returning to Nikita's apartment.

"What the hell! You scared me," Nikita screamed as she found Rahul standing at the door of her bedroom with his arms crossed. "Really? I thought you wouldn't even notice if a burglar came in while your romantic phone calls are going on," Rahul spoke through clenched teeth, trying to control his anger. "It is just a friend from the office and we were not being romantic..." Nikita's voice trailed off as Rahul pulled her, trying to grab the phone. After a minute of struggle, she lost the phone to him.

"Are you serious? This guy, really?" Rahul's anger showed no signs of subsiding. "Do you have any self-respect? A guy who basically called you a joke, is now your midnight call buddy? Are you even dating him now? Moreover, I can't believe you've been lying to my face for this guy. Does our friendship mean nothing to you? What has he done to gain such a top priority in your life that you're ready to throw your relationships under the bus for him?" His tirade was interrupted by an incoming call from Rajeev. Nikita lunged to snatch the phone back, desperation in her eyes.

Nikita screamed as he cut the call, "Why did you do that? Now he's going to get angry and won't talk to me for days. I'll have to spend all my time apologizing now. You have no idea about the extent of his rage." She sat down dejectedly, and Rahul, calming down a bit, embraced her. "I know exactly about this anger, and that's why I can't understand why you've started talking to him again when you don't work with him anymore. The whole point of the new job was to avoid this guy, and now you've made him your best buddy."

Nikita lay down on the bed, still holding onto Rahul's hand. "You don't know him. He's helping me navigate this corporate life. I don't have a mentor, and both you and Priya are in completely different industry. I don't know anyone or anything in consulting, and he's just holding my hand as I find my way through it. That's all."

Rahul lay down beside her, patting her head as she nestled in his arms. "I don't want you to get emotionally attached to such a heartless guy again. You know how protective I am about you. I don't want to see you cry like you did last time because of Rajeev."

Nikita murmured as she drifted off to sleep, "You're there for me, I know. If he hurts me again, you'll always be there for me." Rahul smiled as he hugged her until she fell asleep, completely forgetting about Priya, who was still awake in his flat, looking at the clock and noting that an hour had passed since he had asked her to leave.

In the morning, Priya was treated to Rahul's special pancakes, expecting an apology for the previous night. Instead, Rahul went on and on about how Nikita was still in touch with her old boss. "He doesn't even remember that he forgot about me last night and is least bothered about my feelings. His 24/7 obsession with Nikki needs to be kept in check, and that Nikki also needs to learn her boundaries," Priya mused, staring angrily at Rahul as he cooked.

"We have to attend Rakshit's music launch party today. There's also a pre-party meetup, so you can start getting ready and save your Nikki stories for the party," Priya said, getting up to leave, her ears hurting from his endless talk about Nikita. Little did she know, there was more to come.

"I can't. I don't trust Nikki alone here. She'll start chatting with her boss again or, even worse, might go out to meet him. I have to make sure she doesn't make a fool of herself again," Rahul said, moving towards the door with a pile of pancakes.

Priya made one last attempt to control the spiraling situation. "Let's take her to the party. And where are you taking those pancakes? You can eat here while we talk." "I'll eat with Nikki, and your idea is great. I'll tell her to come to the party too. This will keep her mind off her stupid boss," Rahul said, moving out, leaving a teary and desperate Priya alone.

As she watched him walk away, a vivid flashback from her school days surfaced in her mind. She remembered the day Rahul had caught her cheating and her desperate, foolish suggestion of a casual relationship. Back then, she had assumed his love for her was so deep that he would forgive her betrayal and agree to anything to keep her in his life. Little did she know that the same guy, who once seemed hopelessly devoted to her, was now in love with someone as "ordinary" as Nikki—despite having a girlfriend like her. The thought stung more than she cared to admit.

Priya had tolerated Nikki since school because she never thought an ordinary-looking girl like her could be a threat to her relationship with Rahul. But this situation was fast getting out of her hands, and she didn't like it one bit. Rahul's constant attention to Nikki was driving a wedge between them, and the realization that she might lose him to Nikki was becoming all too real.

ELEVEN

DRUNK NIKITA TURNS ROMANTIC

Rakshit, a guy from their school, who despite being good friends with Rahul and Priya, was someone Nikita had hated since their school days. As she congratulated him on his music launch, his reply reminded her exactly why she had disliked him all these years. "Why are you even here? And if you were going to come, you could have asked Priya for better clothes," he sneered.

Before she could respond, Rahul came to her rescue, pulling her away to the VIP lounge. Nikita could never quite fit in with these people, but Rahul always ensured she didn't feel out of place. His gang could never get rid of her because they all knew how protective Rahul was of her. She couldn't recall when his protectiveness started, but it might have been around the time they had pulled a prank on her in school.

Suddenly, Priya came screaming and plopped herself onto Rahul's lap, complaining about some song they should be dancing to. As Rahul left with Priya to hit the dance floor, Nikita finally got some privacy to message Rajeev.

Rajeev had been fuming since the previous night when his phone call had been ignored, and he still hadn't received any explanation from Nikita. He sat in his car, staring at the club entrance where the launch party was going on, wracking his brain for an excuse to go inside without revealing that he had been stalking her for weeks. Keeping her out of his mind, had been nearly impossible; he needed to know every detail of her activities. Philip had already chided him for becoming a psychotic lover, so Rajeev had to manage this obsession on his own.

Finally, his phone buzzed with a message from Nikita: "Where are you? I'm at a stupid party and missing you badly." This was the excuse he needed. He quickly called her to get the exact address, waited a few more minutes in his car to make it seem less suspicious, and then got out, ready to use the alibi that he was in the vicinity for some work.

Nikita and Rakshit were busy gazing at Rahul and Priya's dance moves on the floor. Trying to distract himself, Rakshit taunted Nikita, "Now that you've started earning, how long do you still plan on cashing in on Rahul's scholarship friendship and charity rent?" Nikita shot back, "As soon as you start making some money off your flop music and stop living off your dad's inheritance." She turned towards the club door when she saw Rajeev entering.

"You're here! But how? I just sent you the message," an excited Nikita hugged him and pulled him towards the bar. Rajeev started explaining how he was in the neighborhood as he ordered two shots. Nikita hesitated, but Rajeev held her mouth and forcefully poured the shot in.

"Ughhhh, that burns! Now I know why I haven't tried it yet. It is just not worth the money. I can drink a liter of cola for a quarter of that cost, and it'll taste better without burning my throat," Nikita managed to say as she asked for tap water to soothe her throat. Rajeev smiled and shook his head. "You're standing at a bar and insulting all the alcohols. You should be banned from entering these clubs if you're going to say cola is better than tequila."

Rahul managed to escape Priya's never-ending dance moves and started searching for Nikita. He was half scared that Rakshit would be annoying her again and she might leave, but it was his turn to be annoyed seeing Rajeev making Nikita drink a shot. He marched towards the bar and chided Nikita, all the while giving death stares to Rajeev.

"What do you think you are doing? You've never even had a proper cocktail and now you're downing shots! Do you want to be sick all day tomorrow? And why is this guy here?" Nikita dragged Rajeev to their lounge, saying, "He's my friend and he's staying. You can continue dancing with your classy friends who didn't even want me here."

Rahul followed behind helplessly, asking, "What happened? Did Rakshit say anything again? You don't have to react to every bit of crap that comes out of his mouth." Before he could calm Nikita down or keep Rajeev away from her, Priya came and pulled him back to the dance floor.

Rahul felt helpless as he tried to manage the growing tension between him and Priya, which had been brewing for days. He couldn't stop glancing over at Nikita and Rajeev, who were getting closer in the lounge.

"You asked me to act all aloof with him, and now look at him romancing Priya. I don't think you're an expert in the love field. I have no idea how you manage to get girls fawning over you," Nikita said, her voice slightly slurred as she started feeling the effects of the alcohol.

"I am an expert on the subject of alcohol, though," Rajeev replied, enjoying the new confident Nikita. "So let me teach you a bit about that. It's considered pathetic by the general public to get drunk after your first shot. You need to work on improving your capacity. Let's slowly start with cocktails." He was relishing this moment, feeling triumphant that she took his side during her fight with Rahul. Although she called him just a friend, he knew he could change that soon.

Nikita's obsession with Rahul seemed to fade with each drink as she tightened her grip on Rajeev's hand and began looking at him endearingly. "Why did you agree to my stupid plan? You don't have to waste time with me. I used to think you hated me at work, but now you're so caring and protective. Do you like me?" Rajeev felt uncomfortable with these questions as she hugged him. He quickly canceled further orders and offered to drop the already tipsy Nikita home.

"I don't want to go home until you tell me the truth. Do you think I'm cute? Do you like me? I know you liked me that day in the hotel, but I don't know what happened after that." Rajeev wasn't ready to confess his feelings for Nikita, not while the Rahul chapter was still open. He stood up and literally pulled her toward the club exit to stop her from asking more prying questions.

"We'll talk when you're sober. Right now, I want to make sure you don't puke all over this club's floor. It seems you've discovered your tolerance limit, which is four drinks,"

Rajeev said, dragging her toward the parking lot.

As soon as he opened the car door, Nikita surprised him by pulling him towards her and kissing him. However, within a second, they were both startled by an unexpected interruption—a shove from Rahul.

Rahul's eyes never lost sight of Nikita, even while he was slow dancing with Priya. When he saw a barely-able-to-stand Nikita leaving with Rajeev, he seized the opportunity to escape Priya's daily nagging session. He rushed through the crowded club and managed to reach them just in time to see Rajeev seemingly kiss Nikita forcefully. He shoved Rajeev away, grabbing Nikita, "Get the hell off her, dude, or I'll call the police."

Rahul tried to support the tipsy Nikita as he threatened Rajeev, but Nikita clung to Rajeev, mumbling, "Leave him, he didn't do anything. He's my friend. Rahul, go away from here." Priya, Rakshit, and a few friends had gathered around, having seen Rahul rush out. Priya stepped forward to calm the situation and took hold of Nikita.

"Rajeev, you can leave. We'll take Nikki with us. Rahul, please go bring your car around," Priya said. Rahul shot an angry look at Rajeev before heading out to get his car. Rajeev told Priya to call him if Nikita needed anything before driving away.

Rahul put Nikita to bed, still shouting at Priya, "I don't understand why you had to come in between. Couldn't you see what he was trying to do with her? She's your friend, and you seem to be least bothered about what was happening to her and more worried about your party being interrupted."

"You're overreacting. She just had a few drinks, and that guy was just trying to help her get home safely. Will you stop being overprotective? She's a grown-up, and you're acting like her dad," Priya replied with frustration. Rahul placed a bucket near Nikita and tucked her in, then turned to Priya, "Can you just leave for now? Let me deal with one thing at a time. She's already sick."

As Priya left, Rahul moved toward the door, but Nikita caught his hand. "Please don't be angry with me. You are my only f riend. I love you," she murmured before falling back on the bed and passing out. Rahul returned to her side and gave her a gentle hug. "Nikki, I won't let anything happen to you ever. I'll punch any guy who even thinks about coming close to you; because you're mine," he whispered.

Nikita heard his words but kept her eyes closed, not wanting to ruin the moment or scare him away. Despite her efforts to remain still, she couldn't help but smile as she hugged him back, her heart swelling with hope and affection.

TWELVE

MISSION RAHUL IS A SUCCESS.. OR MAYBE NOT

Nikita woke up to her doorbell ringing continuously. She realized she was severely hungover and had a bad headache, the moment she opened her eyes. Fumbling towards the door, she assumed Rahul had forgotten his keys again but was surprised to find Rajeev standing there instead. Conscious of her disheveled hair and very short nightdress, she was caught off guard when a worried-looking Rajeev suddenly hugged her.

"I am so sorry. I didn't know you would get this sick. I kept calling you all morning, but you didn't answer, and it worried me even more, so I had to come here," Rajeev said, his voice filled with concern.

Nikita glanced at the clock, which showed it was already one in the afternoon, and felt her headache intensify. She gently asked Rajeev to sit in the living room while she went inside to change into her overalls.

"I am fine now. I'm just not used to drinking so much. I hope I didn't do anything inappropriate, as Rahul was quite pissed off at me," Nikita laughed as she handed Rajeev his favorite black coffee. "You don't remember what happened?" Rajeev wanted clarification on her behavior but was cut off by an ecstatic and babbling Nikita.

"You know, the best part was that Rahul got so jealous he even fought with Priya for me. I don't think he has ever put me above Priya. It has always been about how Priya is right and I should let things go whenever we have fights, but yesterday was all about me," she said, falling onto Rajeev's lap. Rajeev's hand instinctively went to caress her hair as she gleefully recounted the events involving Rahul. He listened, but all he could focus on was the happy Nikita, completely trusting him and feeling so comfortable in his presence.

Rajeev's eyes could have stared into Nikita's eyes forever if Rahul had not barged in, immediately launching into the same tirade from the night before. "Nikki, what are you doing? What is wrong with you? Why are you sleeping in his lap? And you," he pointed an accusatory finger at Rajeev, "I told you to stay the hell away from Nikki. If you try to come anywhere close to her again, I'm calling the police. Just get out of my house right now."

Rajeev gave one last look to a terrified Nikita, who seemed too dumbstruck to speak, before storming out of the flat. Rahul then turned towards Nikita, fury and disbelief in his eyes. "What were you thinking? You hardly know that guy, and you're ready to jump in bed with him? I had no idea you'd become that desperate." "I didn't do anything, and he is a nice guy," Nikita wailed as she ran into the bedroom, tears streaming down her face.

Rahul started pacing in the living room, trying to calm himself before heading towards the bedroom in search of Nikita. He found her lying on the bed, crying profusely. He gently caressed her hair. "Nikki, you have no idea what guys are like. You may consider him a friend, but all guys expect one thing in return for their friendship." Nikita cut him off, shouting through her tears, "You don't know him, and I was telling him about how much I like you, you idiot!"

Rahul was taken aback, as always, by Nikita's upfront confession. It reminded him of the time in school when she had suddenly come to him and told him how she liked him. He smiled and lay down beside Nikita. "I've known that since school, but why make these sudden confessions to random guys? If you need to talk or vent, I should be your only 'go to' person. I don't want you to trust any loser guys because they will take advantage of your naïve nature."

"What am I supposed to tell you? How much I love my roommate's boyfriend? How the only solace I get is when I'm in your arms? How you manage to solve all my problems magically, and how I want you to keep doing that for me forever? Yes, let's have this 'not at all' awkward discussion. What do you want to know?" Nikita vented as she rolled over to hug Rahul.

Rahul smiled as he hugged her back. "You know you're my best friend, and whenever you need me, I'll be there for you before you even have to ask. I've shared things with you that I haven't even shared with Priya. What else do you want? I know I'm in an open relationship, but I can't declare that I'm dating you. I'm not sure how Priya will react, and you're very different from the people my family is used to hanging out with. My parents already love Priya, and they expect me to date someone from their society, if not her. I can't just put someone like you in front of them. They're too image-conscious. What's wrong with the relationship we have right now? Have I ever stopped you from getting close to me? I just don't want to create a furor that will happen if we date publicly."

Nikita had been insulted by class and status many times by Rahul's friends, but hearing these words come from Rahul himself as an explanation for why he couldn't date her, felt incredulous. She couldn't take it anymore and got up from the bed, feeling disgusted—more with herself than with Rahul—for spilling out her feelings to him. Rahul was still speaking about how much he cared for her and how he couldn't see her get hurt by other guys, so he protected her, but Nikita had zoned out, lost in memories of school when she had been insulted by Rahul's gang of friends for her often-disheveled, non-branded clothes and ungroomed look.

Rahul came and hugged her, saying, "I will give you everything you want so you won't need any other guy in your life, but don't ask for this girlfriend tag, please. You need to ditch this old-fashioned 'love-forever' mindset and act like a carefree, fun girl.

After his phone rang for the tenth time, Rahul left, saying that Priya was getting furious. Nikita was too lost in her thoughts to even feel jealous about that. She suddenly remembered how Rajeev had looked at her with disgust when he left and thought to herself that she should try to save at least one relationship in her life. She called Rajeev as she left her house, but he kept disconnecting her calls, giving her a slight indication of how mad he would be. However, it was nothing compared to what she was actually going to witness in person.

THIRTEEN

DEJECTED NIKITA NEEDS A CONFIDANT

Nikita managed to reach Rajeev's house, as he had shared the address once, but looking at the mansion ahead of her, she couldn't believe she was at the right place. She went to the guard and asked if Rajeev was at the house, requesting him to inform Rajeev that Nikita was there.

Rajeev was pacing up and down in frustration, but a smile crept onto his face when he saw Nikita through the camera visuals at his gate. He couldn't believe she had actually come to his house, but he tried to keep a straight face, not wanting to forgive her so easily. When Nikita entered, she seemed her usual chirpy self, showing no signs of regret for what had happened, which triggered Rajeev's anger again.

"Why are you working a 9-5 job in an office when you own such a huge mansion? Do you live here alone?" asked Nikita as she strutted across rooms, marveling at the opulence.

Rajeev's irritation bubbled over. "Why are you here, Nikita? Did you get permission from your Rahul to talk to me? Has he allowed you to be around me and in a stranger's house? I hope he's given you permission to breathe and move around me, or else he'll be calling the cops on me," he said, his voice laced with sarcasm and his teeth gritted.

Nikita turned in fear, sensing Rajeev's anger but unsure how to calm him down. She rushed to hug him and began apologizing profusely. "I didn't know what to do when Rahul suddenly entered. I felt guilty for some unknown reason, and when he told you to get out, I couldn't say anything because it is actually his house. I don't have much right there. But I know it was wrong to call a friend over and let him get insulted. I hope you can forgive me, but I'd understand if you don't want to talk to me again."

Rajeev remained silent; his face still set in a stern expression. Nikita continued, her voice trembling, "Actually, I wanted to tell you in person that you don't have to talk to me again if you don't want to. Mission Rahul is a big flop. He said he liked me but would never date me because I'm not his type. So, if you don't want to see my face again, the good news is you can easily escape, and I won't protest. I don't have any reason to bother you for help anymore. I'm really sorry for my behavior and doubly thankful for yours. You tolerated my dramas for so long."

Rajeev's anger had already melted with the hug, but Nikita's story about Rahul made him concerned for her again. He made her sit close to him, caressing her back, and asked for the details. She shrugged and hugged him again, mumbling, "There's not much to tell. Basically, he was jealous and possessive because of you, so I told him about my feelings. He gave a long lecture on how important

I am to him, even more than Priya, but still he can't date me because I'm from a different society."

Rajeev fidgeted a little hearing this confession from Rahul, but Nikita seemed not to have grasped its full meaning, and he didn't want to clarify it for her. Nikita turned to lay her head on Rajeev's lap, her eyes swelling with tears as she continued, "Basically, he said I'm too down-market, poor, and ugly to qualify as his girlfriend. Anyway, I just wanted to apologize for my behavior this morning and tell you about the failed Mission Rahul, so if you don't want to talk to me, you don't have to."

Rajeev felt like he had won the battle without having fought it, but he also knew the victory was short-lived. Nikita could easily be swayed by Rahul, especially since it was clear that Rahul liked her more than a friend. "For the future, I have a couple of rules. Rule number one: I don't want to go to a house where I might be thrown out, so if we meet, it will be only at this house. Rule number two: I am not a backup option for someone who turns to me only after being rejected elsewhere. If you're okay with these two rules, then we can continue to talk," Rajeev said as he caressed her forehead while she lay on his lap.

Nikita looked up at him in surprise and replied, "You are not a backup. You are so different from my usual friend circle. I can talk to you without being judged for money or looks. Look at you; you're wearing the most boring white and black nightwear. Rahul and Priya would wear branded, colorful pajamas just in case some paparazzi spotted them. The pretense is tiring sometimes, but I guess that's the life of showbiz. I feel so free of judgment and peer pressure when I'm with you. Also, I need you badly to vent about Rahul and Priya. My so-called friend circle is really more of a high-society clique, and I was forcefully inducted into it."

Rajeev relaxed a little; it didn't seem like Nikita was going anywhere soon. Listening to her voice and stories was soothing to him, so he asked more prying questions, "I fail to understand, if you keep saying you're different from them and they keep insulting you, then why are you even with them?"

Nikita took his hand and intertwined her fingers with his as she replied, "It's a long story. They ragged me a lot in school because I came from a different economic background than theirs, or perhaps they just saw me as some strange creature from a different society, but one day, Rahul suddenly felt guilty about their behavior toward me. From that day onwards, he was extra nice to me and even made all his friends be nice to me. He realized they took pranks too far and wanted to make up for it, I guess. Their families are in show business, so when Rahul found out I was planning to take an education loan for college, he offered me small roles in a few music videos to make money. I guess he's been taking care of me since school, so I became their friend.It's not that I didn't try making friends outside this group, but it was the most popular groupin school, and it would've been foolish of me not to join when I had the chance. However there were a few negatives. Everyone saw me as an entry ticket into this popular gang. Especially guys who would befriend me; they would only use me as a stepping stone to get acquainted with Priya or Rahul. Hence, here we are."

Rajeev was now even more curious since Philip had not provided such detailed information about Nikita; her school life and the beginning of the Rahul story were still a mystery to him. He kept probing, "What was this prank that made Rahul feel so guilty that he devoted his life to compensating by taking care of you?"

Nikita, sleepy and half-dozing, shrugged off the question. "I don't know. He pulled a lot of pranks, so it's difficult to know which specific one made him guilty. I'll tell you later about the pranks and ragging stories. Can I sleep for a while before I have to go back and listen to Rahul's 101 reasons not to date me?"

Rajeev nodded, patting her head to help her sleep, while he himself drifted off, thinking about how to get Rahul out of their lives.

FOURTEEN

RAHUL CAN'T CHOOSE

Rahul shook his head in anger as he saw Nikita get out of Rajeev's car. He glanced at the clock striking ten and looked back at the window, watching Nikita struggle to free herself from Rajeev's hand on the dark, pitch-black road. He stood at the door as Nikita entered, giggling to herself. She stepped back and stared in shock at him.

"What are you doing here at night? Are you ever at your own apartment?" Nikita asked as she moved toward the kitchen. "At least I'm at one of my houses, which you don't seem to be using anymore. I'm thinking about moving in here with Priya," Rahul replied with a smirk.

Nikita felt a pang of guilt as she set down the water bottle and tried to find an answer. "I was with an office mate, had some work to finish, and didn't notice it had gotten so late."

Rahul sat down, frustration boiling over, and nearly pulled his hair out as he shouted, "Will you for once stop lying to me? Do you think I'm blind and can't see Rajeev dropping you off? What are you trying to do? Make a fool out of two guys? Is it not enough that you're making a fool out of me that you need another one?"

Nikita, irritated by his accusations, blurted out, "How am I making you a fool? You clearly told me I'm too ugly and classless to date. Rajeev has already rejected me because I don't meet his standards for a girlfriend. I think my situation should enter the world record of sorts where I've been dumped by two guys in less than six months without even dating either of them. So please, explain to me how I'm making a fool of you? Anyways, I'm tired, so I'm going to sleep. You think about it and give me an answer tomorrow. Please leave."

Nikita moved towards the bedroom, leaving Rahul dumbstruck. He followed her, trying to give her some convincing explanations, "I didn't dump you, and I don't think you're ugly or classless. Where did you get this idea? I was telling you how I've fallen for you even when you're so different from the people I've usually dated. I tried to stop falling in love with you, telling myself how different you are from me, but I was helpless."

Nikita stared at him in disbelief before smirking, "Yes, that's a much better explanation. You didn't want to fall in love with someone as low-grade as me. If it's that painful for you, then you shouldn't be around me. I don't even understand why you are friends with me since it can be quite embarrassing for you in public."

Rahul tried to hold her as he pleaded, "You're taking it out of context. I did not plan this. I never understood how important you became to me. I just can't stand the thought of you giving anyone else more importance than me. I kept telling myself that you're just a friend and not my type, but I guess I do like you."

Nikita's hand unconsciously went to Rahul's cheek, caressing it to comfort him. "What do you want from me, Rahul? I don't get you. We are friends and always will be. I am there for you when you need me, and I will disappear when you feel embarrassed. Is that okay?"

Rahul's eyes filled with tears as he held Nikita even tighter. "You don't embarrass me. Will you stop saying that?" He was interrupted by his phone ringing, and Priya's name flashed on the screen. Nikita got up to leave, saying, "You should pick up Priya's call. You won't be able to explain why you are here."

Rahul held her hand and typed a quick message as he spoke, "I just want to be with you tonight. Can we just forget about it for now and solve this issue tomorrow?" Nikita smiled as she embraced him, resting her head on his chest while Rahul kissed her forehead.

It was already seven when Nikita woke up and couldn't find Rahul in her bed. She freshened up, but there was still no trace of Rahul in the entire flat, so she decided to check his flat next door. As she entered, she found Rahul making pancakes in the kitchen, looking adorable in his apron. She hugged him as she spoke, "Where did you disappear this morning?"

Rahul shrugged off her hands immediately as Priya entered, rubbing her eyes. "Rahul, can you keep the noise down in the kitchen? I slept so late yesterday because of you and your late-night jokes. I'm already tired from yesterday's shoot and your shenanigans. Nikki, what are you doing here so early in the morning? Am I the only night owl around here?"

Nikita was left speechless by Priya's comments and looked at Rahul in shock. Rahul tried to salvage the situation, saying, "She wanted to eat, and her fridge didn't have much left, so she came here. I think she smelled my pancakes and just made up a lame excuse." Priya and Rahul laughed as Priya took a banana and replied, "Fine, you two keep it quiet. I'm going back to sleep. Rahul doesn't let me sleep, Nikki."

Nikita smiled at Priya and waited patiently until her bedroom door closed before turning her scathing eyes toward Rahul. "So, you were hugging me at night and then left in the middle of the night to do all that with Priya? What is wrong with you? After all that nonsense about liking me, you didn't take even minutes to flip. Ok, I need to sit down; my head hurts."

Rahul tried to calm Nikita down, glancing nervously toward the bedroom. "Will you speak softly? I haven't talked to Priya yet about us. She came back late yesterday, so I couldn't bring it up. I just need some time to sort things out before I bombard her with these issues." Nikita looked up angrily and gave him a kick on the shin. "Yes, it was not too late to do that but too late to talk."

As Nikita left, Priya went back to her bed, having overheard the entire conversation through her bedroom door. She closed her eyes as she heard Rahul enter, but he went out again after checking if she was asleep. She wasn't ready for a confession from him. Priya made up her mind to put a stop to this budding love story. She tried to sleep but kept tossing and turning in anger.

FIFTEEN

THE SCHOOL FLASHBACK

Rajeev felt like pulling his hair out as Nikita rambled on about Rahul. He decided to put a stop to it. "So, you're telling me that Rahul loves you but also loves Priya. He'll continue being in a relationship with Priya and will also date you behind her back. And you think this is a great victory for you? Well, then, congratulations are in order! You've officially become his doormat. "

Nikita stopped playing with Rajeev's hand and got up angrily from the sofa, where just a few minutes ago she was happily telling her love story.

"I thought you were my friend and would understand me," Nikita defended Rahul, her voice trembling. "No one has treated me nicer than Rahul. He actually likes to talk to me, unlike other guys who just wanted to use me to get close to Priya. Rahul is the only one who likes me without any ulterior motive. He has done a lot for me since school and even now. You have no idea."

Rajeev smirked as he settled down on the sofa, crossing his legs. "Please, enlighten me then about Rahul baba. Tell me more about his greatness that makes you so desperate for him."

"Stop smirking. Rahul is very protective about me. He never gets as caring even for Priya. In school, he had ragged me initially along with his friends, but then he felt guilty after an incident and became intensely protective. He literally scans the history of any guy I try to date, even you. He told me to stay away from you because of your history of hookups with strangers, but I just didn't listen to him..."

Nikita's voice trailed off as Rajeev's anger flared. "Excuse me? What hookups and what strangers? You and Rahul have no idea about my history or anything else. He's feeding you nonsense, and you, like his domesticated pet, lap up whatever he says," Rajeev lashed out.

Nikita impulsively hugged him to calm him down, speaking softly, "He just meant that you're not the serious kind of guy that I was looking for, who could become my forever love. He knows me better than I know myself, so I trust him when he says you're not what I would want."

Normally, her hug would have calmed him down, but today his anger spiraled out of control. He pushed her away hard, his voice rising, "So Rahul tells you what kind of guy you should want? Does he also tell you what to eat and what to say? This is progress—from doormat to puppet. And what kind of guy do you both think I am? If you and Rahul think so poorly of me, what are you doing in my house every day? You should stay away from me; otherwise, as per your Rahul, I might do despicable things to the innocent you."

Nikita was on the verge of tears as she tried to explain herself, "I don't think so now, specially after we became friends. He used to say these things before, and he says all this about every guy. Most of the time, he's right, so I used to listen to him, but with you, I just feel safe."

She hugged him again as she spoke, "When I'm with you, it feels like all my problems will get solved. You're not interested in useless things like other guys were, and especially, you're not interested in Priya, which is a huge relief." She smiled and looked at him, seeing his anger start to subside a bit.

Rajeev patted her and made her sit with him on the sofa, but he still couldn't get Rahul out of his mind. "Why is he so overprotective of you? He doesn't want to date you, but he doesn't let you date anyone else. This is a little difficult to follow. I still don't get how you joined his gang of friends in school since none of them seem to like you, nor do you seem to like them. What happened in your school that you couldn't make better friends than these guys? Were you really into Rahul, or did you just want a role in his music videos? I can't think of a third reason."

Nikita took his hand as she leaned on him and said, "I think he just feels guilty for ragging me initially. He and his friends made my life a living hell in school. Then he felt bad and tried overcompensating by becoming overprotective. It's all a very long and boring story which might make you hate Rahul a little more, so let it be."

"It's a Saturday, and frankly, I have nothing else to do. I need more reasons to hate that self-righteous dude," Rajeev said as he caressed Nikita's hair, wondering why she was so comfortable with him yet still managed to talk only about Rahul.

Nikita settled comfortably, holding Rajeev's hand as she began her story. "Well, I had received a scholarship and just moved to a metro city from a small town, trying to adjust to the new school and the kids around. It was already difficult, but mean teenagers made the situation worse. My shabby look and pretentious display of intellect in class did not go well with Rahul and his rich kids' gang, especially Priya.

She was used to being the teacher's pet and was almost the only one with brains in that class, so she didn't like me as competition, especially since I didn't qualify for the high society class standards of that school. Daily taunts about my look became a habit for her and her friends as they followed everything Priya said. But until then, I don't think anyone had a personal problem with me. It mainly started after the exams."

"I saw Rahul cheating in exams," Nikita began, settling comfortably with Rajeev's hand in hers. "He was passing chits around that he had hidden in his shoes. He saw me staring at him and smiled, but I looked away in disgust. I guess I still had that self-righteous attitude of being the scholarship student. I don't know what exactly happened, but the teacher got a whiff of the cheating, either from the answer sheets or because someone ratted him out. Rahul got called to the principal's office later.

In the examination hall, I had seen them cheating so they suspected me of complaining. Rahul and Priya had started working professionally since they were kids and had done a couple of music albums along with web series. They had a huge fan following in school. People were ready to die for Priya and kill anyone for Rahul. That's the kind of aura they had, which in turn made my life a big mess."

"Rahul was in revenge mode, and I was in love mode," Nikita continued. "I guess I was one of the many in school who were starstruck seeing these celebrities so close to me. Plus, my small-town upbringing made me fawn over them. It didn't take much for me to become Rahul's fan girl, so when I saw him cheating in class, his image in my eyes was shattered. However, when he came to talk to me (as part of his revenge), I had a fangirl moment and was back to daydreaming about him."

Rajeev got up, frustrated, and said, "So let me get this straight. He used your crush on him as a tool to make a fool out of you to satisfy his revenge, but you still think he's the good guy?"

Nikita blinked at his outburst and replied, "He didn't use anything. I liked him, and well, it worked in his favor, making his revenge easier. You have to listen to the full story. He felt guilty about it and is still compensating by being protective of me. It isn't his fault that I liked him and he didn't like me back, just as it isn't your fault that I liked you and you didn't like me that way. I just need to stop wearing my heart on my sleeve to avoid getting hurt, but I guess it will take a lot of time for me to learn. I can't stop liking people if they are nice to me."

Rajeev was angry at being compared to Rahul, but he wanted to hear the full story before bursting out again. He didn't like the comparison, but at least now he knew that she liked him as much as she liked Rahul, so he was okay with the tiny steps he was taking. Things would change, but he needed to know what he was up against before he made any move to win. So, he settled back on the sofa, pulling Nikita towards him, and said, "Okay, continue with the story."

SIXTEEN

THE SCHOOL SAGA CONTINUES

As soon as Rahul got out of the principal's office, his gang of friends gathered around to hear the result. "He suspended me for this week, so I can't take any more exams. I have to retake these papers with the next batch of students, but since it's just one subject, I'm not being held back for the year," Rahul assured them.

Priya, however, was still angry. She gritted her teeth as she spoke, "It's that scholarship girl. I am sure she is the one who complained against you. Don't worry, I am going to make her life hell." Rahul remained calm and told them to stay away from her. "She is my problem, and I will solve it."

Rahul waving at her was such a new thing for Nikita that she had to look behind her to check if he was waving at someone else. She was sitting alone in the school field, and no one seemed to be around her bench. Rahul approached her, leaving no doubt that he was waving at her, as he said, "Hey, thanks for ratting me out. You got me out of giving exams. You are Nikita, right? Can I call you Nikki?"

Nikita stood up in surprise and replied, "I didn't complain about you. Why would I do that?" Rahul held her hand as she was leaving. "Nikki dear, I'm not complaining. I'm thanking you for helping me escape school for a week. I just came to introduce myself and start this new friendship."

Nikita tried to free her hand again as she replied, "You are mistaken. I have not told anyone about you cheating. I don't even talk to anyone, let alone teachers." Rahul was in no mood to let her escape. "Fine, but what's wrong with getting to know each other, Nikki? Hi, I am Rahul. You would have seen me roaming around the classes but not entering any. I hate studying and love music. You can join our jam sessions in the music club room when you get free time from all your books. Come on, I will show you."

Priya and Rakshit stood up in astonishment as Rahul entered the music room with his arm around Nikita's shoulder. He was showing her around and explaining how they practiced both dance and music there when Priya decided to intervene, "I think she has lost her way. This is not her kind of place. Miss Scholarship should stay away from cheaters like us, otherwise, she'll have to spend a full day complaining to the principal."

Rahul looked at Priya and continued talking to Nikki, "Ignore Pri, she gets a bit hyper now and then. Both she and I are good dancers and can give you a lesson in case you feel like trying extracurricular activities some day. I'd love to teach you since I'm pretty free for the week and will be spending my suspension here. From your quizzical look, I can guess you're wondering why I'm being so friendly. I just like making new friends, and you seemed like you needed one. I haven't seen you interacting with anyone except the librarian, I guess."

Nikita brushed off his arm from around her shoulder and said, "I would love to learn how to dance, but I don't think your friends like me, so it's better if I concentrate in the library with the books instead of the music room. I'd love to be friends, but maybe it's better if we only talk in class." She left the room while Rakshit and Priya glared at her. Rahul could do nothing except look at them with annoyance in his eyes. Priya approached Rahul to reason with him, "I don't understand why you're being nice to the person who got you suspended, but don't expect the same from me." Rahul hugged her and said, "Just chill, babe, and trust me."

Rahul spent the week mostly in the library, trying to make Nikita talk to him, but ended up getting tutored by her instead. "You're quite sharp and know most of the concepts. I don't get why you had to cheat," Nikita said, surprised at the pace at which Rahul was solving the test equations.

"I guess I am lazy and just don't care. I want to be a rockstar, so why bother with math and biology? I don't like to waste my brain on things that don't have... what did you call it? Yes, return on investment," Rahul replied, trying to lean back on the highly uncomfortable library chair.

Nikita smiled as she got up to leave. "I have to go for an exam, but remember, people will be more impressed by a graduate singer than a high school dropout rockstar. When people become your fans, they stalk your entire personal life and judge you on more than just your singing talent. So, become the role model people would love to be fans of." Rahul just watched her leave, too surprised to say anything.

SEVENTEEN

REVENGE PLAN BACKFIRES

Rahul was waiting for Nikita at the school park in the evening. It had become almost a routine for him to hear how her exams went. Nikita came running towards him, beaming from ear to ear. "Exams are over, and the last one turned out to be the best. Tomorrow your suspension will also be over. Can it get better than this?" Rahul smiled at her. She seemed happier about his suspension ending than he was. He impulsively gave her a peck on the cheek. Nikita was shocked, and Rahul quickly apologized, seeing her scared reaction. "I'm sorry. I didn't think it would be a big deal. I'm just used to doing the same with my friends when I'm super happy about something. I'm sorry; now don't get mad."

Nikita blushed hard and turned red as she looked around before she spoke. "It's just that it's my first kiss, and that too from my crush. So, it shocked me a little." "Really? Why didn't you tell me before that I was your crush? I always thought you hated me or thought I was too dumb to converse with because of that cheating incident," Rahul said, putting his arm around her and guiding her to sit on the bench.

"I don't think you're dumb. I love your dancing and have followed all the music videos you've released. I know you're quite intelligent. I'm still surprised about that day because I don't understand why you needed to cheat, but anyway, all that doesn't stop me from crushing on you. Actually, I consider myself quite lucky that I get to be friends with the person I'm a huge fan of; who else gets this opportunity?" Nikita smiled as she intertwined her fingers with his.

Rahul didn't realize it was so late as he bid goodbye to Nikita at her hostel. He smiled to himself, actually enjoying her company. Time seemed to fly when they talked. His thoughts were interrupted as Priya and Rakshit cornered him at the school gate. Priya spoke angrily, "What is up with your snail-paced revenge plan? Or are you on a seven-day dating mission with her? Every day you take the mic and recorder to catch some incriminating evidence, but it finally ends up with nothing. Let us listen to the tape. Maybe neutral ears will find something which your dumb ears have not been able to in the last seven days."

Rahul grasped his bag tightly and refused to part with it. "If I find something, I'll tell you. I told you about my mic recording plan, didn't I? I'll tell you as soon as I get a juicy story from her, and then you'll be part of the next plan, which I have termed 'Nikki's Humiliation.' Now both of you need to go to sleep, and so do I."

Priya was not convinced by Rahul's talk, so as soon as he left, she turned to Rakshit. "Keep an eye on him," she ordered. "Get that recorder. I need to hear what's been cooking up for a week. But be discreet; you know how Rahul gets if we don't do things his way." Rakshit nodded, "Your wish is my command, ma'am."

The next morning, Rahul found a seat near Nikita in class, which irritated Priya to no end. She glanced at the recorder that Rakshit had managed to steal from Rahul's room, then walked out with it, signaling Rakshit to follow. As Nikita was showing Rahul her notes, the school radio announcement started in Priya's voice, "We need to welcome our new scholarship student Nikita, so let's get to know her better. Let's start with the story of her first kiss."

The recorder began playing the conversation Nikita and Rahul had on the bench the previous day. "It's just that it's my first kiss and that too from my crush. So, it shocked me a little."

Nikita looked at Rahul in shock, who was equally surprised. As she looked around, her shock turned to horror at the smirks and mocking glances from her classmates. Rahul ran out of the class to the announcement room, leaving Nikita surrounded by jeering students.

When Rahul reached the radio room, Priya and Rakshit were giggling as the recorder was now playing Rahul's side of the conversation. He cut off the radio and glared at Priya. "What the hell did you do? I told you not to interfere with my plan. You stole the recorder and, without giving any indication, you played this for everyone."

"You looked like you had gone soft on that person who ratted you out, and I had to teach her a lesson which you clearly weren't going to do. I'm not going to apologize for having your back," Priya retorted.

Rahul, fuming, took out the USB with the recordings and ran back to the class to find Nikita. She was nowhere to be seen, but the teacher told him to go immediately to the principal's office as he had been summoned.

Rahul was relieved to see Nikita in the principal's office, but his relief quickly turned to dismay as he heard the principal shouting at her. "I thought you were a bright student. Is this what you have come to this school for? These kids you are hanging out with don't need to study, but you do. Do you want to be involved with such people and lose focus on your studies? I am suspending you for a week, but it is for your own good. Hopefully, the noise around this incident will die down by then, and you can concentrate on your studies instead of wasting time like these star kids do."

Turning to Rahul, the principal continued, "Yes, Mr. Rahul, the same one-week suspension goes for you too. Why were you saving this guy last time, Nikita? Look what he has done. If you had just confessed about what happened on that exam day, I would have given this guy a much more severe punishment, and you wouldn't have to deal with this fiasco. Next time, don't try to protect such idiots as they don't deserve it. Now both of you leave before I increase the suspension term to two weeks."

Rahul was left speechless when he saw the hurt in Nikita's eyes. He realized that apologizing to her was more important than trying to reason with the principal. Taking her hand, he led her to their usual bench. "Look, it was Priya who played that recording. I had no idea until it started playing. I'm sorry for thinking you ratted me out," Rahul explained earnestly.

But before he could finish, Nikita cut him off with a shout, "Is that why you were recording me. All that friendship talks and kiss was a pretense just so that you can trap me into saying something embarrassing and you could use it like this. I told you thousand times that I didn't complain about you. You and your friends are pathetic. Just stay away from me."

Just then, their classmate Akhil walked by and immediately picked up on the tension. He began throwing jeering comments at Nikita. Her disgust was obvious, and Rahul's frustration quickly reached its limit. Acting on impulse, he punched Akhil, feeling a fleeting surge of triumph.

But as he looked up, Nikita was gone. Rahul realized he had only made things worse. He needed to find Nikita and make things right, without any further misunderstandings or confrontations.

EIGHTEEN

THE TRUCE OF THE PAST

The suspension week was finally ending, and it had been a tough competition between Rahul and Nikita over who had it worse. Nikita had endured snarky remarks from both guys and girls about her character wherever she went. The library had become her refuge, while Rahul had cut off all his friends, spending the week sulking and trying to apologize to a stubborn Nikita.

Today marked his nth attempt to ask for forgiveness. He sat across from her in the library, desperation in his voice. "Why can't you believe me that it wasn't my plan to do this? I've already admitted that I was angry because I thought you complained to the principal, so I carried the recorder around. But I swear, in that week, I just grew close to you and dropped the stupid idea of embarrassing you."

Nikita looked at him, her expression weary. "Rahul, I don't care what you wanted to do or what you didn't. The point is, whatever you talked about in those days was all fake, meant to trap me into saying something you could use to your advantage. That entire friendship was fake, so

I don't know what you're trying to do now. I told you; you don't need to ask for forgiveness. I'm not angry or complaining about you to the principal. I've served my suspension and want to put this mess behind me. I was dumb enough to think I was making a friend. You're free to live your life, and let me live mine. There are no hard feelings. Relax. Honestly, I only get angry with people I care about... and I don't think I know you well enough for that. I can't tell what was fake and what wasn't in our short 'friendship,'" Nikita said, standing up to move to a different table.

Rahul was about to follow Nikita to her new table when Priya made an unwelcome entry. He banged his hand on the table in frustration. Priya sat in front of him and whispered, "Why have you been avoiding me? I had to find out from some random person that you're here. What are you doing in a library? Have you lost it? Please don't tell me you're trying to apologize to her. You don't owe her anything."

Rahul shrugged his shoulders and replied, "Pri, just let me be. Stop controlling what I should do and what I shouldn't do. You and Rakshit wanted to do this drama, and now I'm paying for it. Let me pay for it peacefully. If you had a misconception that you did this for me, remove that from your mind because you did it only for your enjoyment. You have a personal problem with Nikki; I don't." He got up to go to Nikita, but she was nowhere to be seen in the library.

As Rahul roamed around the school in search of Nikita, the guard at the gate handed him a courier. He looked at it and took it to a bench in the garden area, usually neglected by the school crowd, so he could peacefully open the package. He looked inside, then around, and let out a scream, "What the Hell!" He stopped suddenly as he saw Nikita staring at him from the corner.

After they were done staring at each other for what felt like an eternity to Rahul, he decided to explain, "I just got something from my parents that I was sort of expecting, but it still irritates me a lot when I see it, so the cussing happened without thinking."

He paused for her reaction, but seeing her still stare at him quizzically, he continued, "My parents send me these birthday gifts as a consolation for never meeting me. Lots of drafts, cheques will come in parts with long instructions on where to spend just to showcase that they care about me but don't care enough to bother showing up for my birthday or anything. So, it is just one of those days again."

Nikita came and sat near him on the bench as she asked, "So what's the issue? You get to buy things that make you happy, which is basically what they want. If you showed them that you didn't need this iPhone or that expensive recorder that you used on me, then maybe they would stop sending you money. All they see is you getting happy with these expensive things, so they want to give you even more. And to earn more, they need to work more. You can't have it both ways."

Rahul smirked as he replied, "Yes, it's my fault that my parents don't like spending time with me on my birthday because I like to use an iPhone. Thanks for the pep talk, ma'am. Why don't you replace our school therapist? Our school needs more psychologists like you to help the kids deal with their issues."

Nikita got up to leave. "I can't meet my parents because we can't afford to travel by plane, but I'm sure they love me and they send me money to buy my things. I'm sure your parents love you too, and that's why they send you money to buy another iPhone or some other useless crap with no questions asked. Stop playing the victim, as a lot of people would kill to be in your position right now." Rahul kept staring at her as she left and then turned to look back at the gift. There was a birthday card with 'Rahul, love you a lot! Have fun!' written on it, which finally made him smile.

Rahul turned around only to find Priya coming towards him. He moved swiftly to follow Nikita, who seemed to be talking to some guy. As he approached them, all he could hear was the guy cracking a joke about the radio incident, and before another word could come out of his mouth, Rahul's punch hit his jaw. Rahul shouted in the hall, "Anyone who cracks a joke about that radio announcement or makes any sly remark to Nikki will face the same. You mess with her; you mess with me."

With this declaration, he smiled and turned to face Nikki, but she had disappeared. Priya was now standing near him. He made a face and tried to leave, but Priya held his hand and said, "I hated her because of what she did to you. I did it all to take revenge for you. If this is what you want now, then I will back off. Don't fight for these silly things. For me, that girl doesn't even exist. Can we please call it a truce now?" Rahul nodded absently and hurried off to find Nikita again

Priya saw him leave but decided not to tell him that she had seen Nikita enter the washroom and instead followed her there. Priya entered the washroom, only to find Nikita staring at the mirror and sobbing. Priya came and held her shoulders, whispering, "This is just a trailer. In case you hit on Rahul again, I will make sure these tears never stop. I sincerely hope for your own good that you don't think Rahul is going to go for a classless personality like yours. I really care for you and wouldn't like to see you hurt, so ciao for now!! Take care and please don't try to go for something that is just too outside your reach."

Nikita washed her face and tried to compose herself as she walked out of the washroom and almost collided with Rahul. "Hey, I was looking for you. My parents' love will be shown through the new watches that I will buy with their money. I just wanted to show you a few as I thought I will give you one too. You know, as a sorry from my side," Rahul said, smiling as he had finally found her after searching around for a long time.

Nikita pushed away his phone and replied angrily, "Do you think I am as materialistic as you and your useless friends? If you want to say sorry, then stay away from me because your girlfriend is threatening me. I just want to study without any drama in my life, so please make sure you and your friends leave me alone. That will be the biggest sorry gift for me."

Rahul was not ready to lose his friendship to another of Priya's dramas, so he dragged Nikita back to their garden bench. "I will make sure that Priya or anyone else does not trouble you. In return, you have to promise to keep tutoring me. If you are okay with this deal, then it's fine; otherwise, let alone others, I will keep troubling you until you forgive me. Your choice," Rahul said, extending his hand.

Nikita stared at him for a long time and then looked around. Finally she shrugged and shook his hand as she replied, "Fine, just tutoring then, so that even if you decide to record me again, it will help you in your daily lessons and nothing more. At your end, you need to make sure your friends stay away from me." Rahul chuckled, shook her hand to seal the deal, then playfully tapped her head before settling beside her on their favorite bench. Priya, arms crossed, watched them intently from the pathway above the garden.

NINETEEN

RAJEEV AND RAHUL GET POSSESSIVE

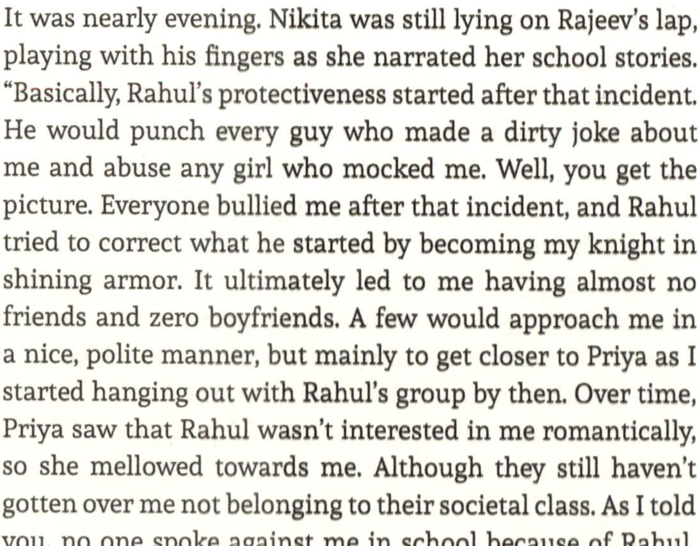

It was nearly evening. Nikita was still lying on Rajeev's lap, playing with his fingers as she narrated her school stories. "Basically, Rahul's protectiveness started after that incident. He would punch every guy who made a dirty joke about me and abuse any girl who mocked me. Well, you get the picture. Everyone bullied me after that incident, and Rahul tried to correct what he started by becoming my knight in shining armor. It ultimately led to me having almost no friends and zero boyfriends. A few would approach me in a nice, polite manner, but mainly to get closer to Priya as I started hanging out with Rahul's group by then. Over time, Priya saw that Rahul wasn't interested in me romantically, so she mellowed towards me. Although they still haven't gotten over me not belonging to their societal class. As I told you, no one spoke against me in school because of Rahul, and that continued even after school."

Rajeev shook his head and spoke with a smirk, "Let me get this straight. That guy started all the drama of insulting you, then made sure you ended up with no friends, and you think he did you a favor? I think he was pretty successful in his plan of taking revenge on you. Just when I think you can't get any dumber, you prove me wrong."

Nikita got up angrily and shouted, "You don't know him as well as I do. He is very caring and protective of me. His parents own a production company and handle most of his music releases. They could easily hire top models for their videos, but when Rahul found out I was planning to take an education loan for my MBA, he offered me roles in a few music videos. He even made sure, after discussing it with the production team, that I would shoot only the scenes I was comfortable with, wear only what I felt good in, and do dance steps that weren't too complicated. He ensured everything was perfect according to my convenience, and I was able to pay for my college."

"Maybe they just got an amateur model like you at a lower cost compared to others who they usually worked with. They knew you wouldn't negotiate and had no grasp of industry dynamics, so they could easily manipulate you," Rajeev brushed off her stories about Rahul's kindness.

However, Nikita refused to give up and kept following him as Rajeev moved to the kitchen for water. "I literally knew nothing except my school books. Rahul took the time to teach me dance and a bit of acting so that I wouldn't screw up the music videos. There was a kissing scene in the video, and when he heard I had never dated a guy, he talked me through it so that I wouldn't feel awkward when the actual shooting happened," Nikita explained, rambling on incessantly without even pausing to take a breath.

Rajeev stopped in his tracks and turned around as he said, "Wait, so that guy jumped on the chance to become the first guy you ever kissed when he could have easily removed that scene from the video since it was his home production. Wow, I have newfound respect for this guy and his admirable methods of making out with women without them even realizing it."

Nikita was angry as she pulled Rajeev's shirt and shouted, "You are making everything sound so sleazy and cunning about Rahul's intentions."

Rajeev slowly removed her hands and replied in a very calm voice, "Yes, I am saying exactly what they are. I don't understand the relationship between Priya and Rahul, but I am pretty sure about you and Rahul now. You are a backup for Rahul, with Priya as the front-end. Maybe Priya does not give him the time and attention for his emotional rants, but they have multiple common interests and look perfect as a pair for their industry. So, at least for business reasons, they won't break up. He actually does not need to break up because that emotional gap is being fulfilled by you, where he dumps all his tantrums on you, and you act as his personal counselor. You both are equally necessary in his life, and he has mastered the art of not letting both of you go by cooking up dumb stories that you both fall for completely, hook, line, and sinker."

Nikita came really close to him and muttered angrily, "You are wrong about Rahul, and I will prove it." She stormed out of his house, her anger palpable, never once looking back.

Rahul was pacing up and down in frustration in Nikita's flat when she unlocked the door and shrieked in surprise, "My God, Rahul! Are you ever in your own flat? Priya spends more time in your flat than you do."

"Which flat are you spending your time in because you haven't been in this one since morning; even refusing to pick up any calls," Rahul leaned against the wall as he asked her, staring continuously with a piercing gaze.

"I was with Rajeev, and before you scream anything, please understand that I have only two close friends in my life that I talk with, and one of them is pretty new, so I spend a little extra time with him – end of story," Nikita replied as she put her arms around Rahul's shoulders. But he refused to calm down and shrugged them off.

Before Rahul could chide her further, Priya entered and looked at him in surprise, "Rahul, I have been looking for you all over. And where were you, Nikki, since morning? If you are going out, then you should tell me. I needed some things from the market."

She paused, looking at the tense scene in the room where both Rahul and Nikita were staring at the floor, avoiding each other's glances. "What's up? Did you both fight again, or did Rahul give some more unsolicited advice on how to live life?" Priya asked Nikki as she pulled her into an embrace.

Rahul couldn't stop himself and blurted out, "I stopped giving advice to you long ago, especially after you chose Rakshit over me, and I will stop doing that for Nikki as well from now on. Even after repeatedly telling her there is a ditch full of filth, she jumps into it anyway."

Rahul left the apartment in anger, leaving behind two confused but stubborn girls. Priya was getting a sense of built-up jealousy in Rahul, but she was not ready to lose to anyone, let alone Nikita. Nikita didn't like upsetting Rahul, but she was not ready to choose between Rahul and Rajeev; at least not yet, as for the first time in her life, she felt happy and safe, and she was not going to give up on it.

TWENTY

PRIYA SUPPORTS NIKKI

Priya had been observing for days how Rahul grew restless every time Nikita went to meet Rajeev. Her patience was wearing thin as Rahul began losing interest in any conversation with her if Nikita wasn't around. Finally, she couldn't hold back any longer and confronted him, "What is going on? Please, no more stories about how concerned you are about Nikki."

"I want an honest conversation because I have known you since childhood and I know your behavior with every girl you've dated. You date them for a while, but you always come back to me. Even when you're dating them, you never give anyone attention if I'm around. But this is going way beyond my understanding. Don't play with me, and don't you dare bring up the same – oh, but you chose this life. Why have you become so obsessed with Nikki's love life?" Priya frantically asked.

Rahul came out of his thoughts but was still speechless as Priya started to understand his behavior while he was still trying to make sense of the situation at hand. He had no answers but, to escape her glares, he decided to go on the attack mode instead of defending himself. "I thought we stopped asking these loyalty-related questions the day you cheated on me with Rakshit. You both parade around me every day and then give me a lecture on how I should put you as my top priority. A bit hypocritical, don't you think?"

Priya got up and managed to put on a fake, frustrated smile as she replied, "All these character attacks on me, only confirm my suspicions that you have fallen for Nikki or maybe have always liked her, but I refused to believe it due to my own love-struck stupidity. We have always been there for each other, no matter how many other relationships we've been in, because we genuinely enjoy each other's company. But now, I just feel like the platonic connection we shared is being stolen by Nikita, and the worst part is that she's winning against me without even knowing she's in the race."

Rahul had never seen Priya so emotionally drained. He always found her to be in command of their relationship, but for the first time, she seemed to be giving up. "Look, I just said that out of frustration. Do you really see me dating Nikita? She is not even close to the type of girls that I have dated, and still, you have such doubts. I don't know why I am even clarifying these things. I thought we were better at understanding each other than other couples, but you have disappointed me today. When people used to ask me how our relationship works, I used to proudly say that it works perfectly for us because we trust each other completely. What should I tell them now?"

Priya blushed at his heartfelt speech and felt a pang of guilt, so she hugged him tightly while saying, "Sorry, it's just that I feel Nikki is still not over the school crush she had on you. I know over the years we have become friends, but she is much closer to you, and I get a little jealous when you both discuss things that I am not part of. However, I am sorry. I understand you and trust you."

Rahul hugged her back, but Priya saw his lost eyes in the mirror, and she just couldn't shake off her suspicion. She needed to not only find out but make sure that even if her suspicion was true, it wouldn't stay true for long. She had been taking 'care' of girls obsessed with Rahul since school and had become somewhat of a pro at solving such issues before they became a problem. She just needed a little help, and who better to go to than the person who started the problem: Nikita's boss, whose entry into Nikita's life had caused havoc in all of theirs.

They heard the flat door open, indicating that Nikita had come back, and Rahul sprang into action, moving towards the door. It took him a few seconds to remember his conversation with Priya, which froze him in his tracks. Priya smiled and said, "Let me check on her as I don't want you to unnecessarily scream at her without knowing the full situation, and you seem in no mood to listen to her at the moment."

Priya found Nikita lying on the sofa, playing with the TV remote when she entered the flat. "I thought both of you had work today. What are you doing at home?" Nikita asked as she got up. "We have to leave in some time for the shoot. There was some delay from the production team. Where have you been?" Priya asked, lying down on the sofa beside her. Nikita looked down, trying to avoid Priya's gaze, and mumbled, "Out with a friend."

Priya sighed, held her hand, and said, "I'm not Rahul, so you don't have to lie to me. I hope you know what you're doing because that guy has been very clear from the start about what he expects from a relationship. I don't want you to have different expectations. Last time, it took us a week and a million Starbucks frappes to bring your smile back. I have a feeling that you're just acting rebellious because Rahul is refusing to let you meet the guy, or maybe you're trying to make Rahul jealous. I hope I'm wrong and this is an actual no-strings-attached relationship because whatever you may think of me, I don't want to see you hurt again like last time."

Nikita was a little surprised at how much Priya had started understanding her and even more surprised by the concern she showed. "You've got me all wrong. I'm not trying to make anyone jealous. Rajeev and I aren't even in a relationship. We just like hanging out together, and since Rahul made quite a scene when he came here last time, I meet him at his house without telling Rahul. That's all; there's no other conspiracy developing here," Nikita gave a half-hearted explanation, hoping Priya would believe it and drop the idea that she was actually trying to make Rahul jealous.

Priya shrugged, not wanting to argue about something she was sure of, but she still needed access to Rajeev to bring her own plan into motion. Whatever feelings were developing between Rahul and Nikita had to be nipped in the bud, and Rajeev had to help her, so she kept pampering Nikita, caressing her hair while she asked, "Why are you scared of Rahul? Invite Rajeev to our parties, and I'll make sure no issues happen. Your friend should be part of our gang too, right?"

Nikita scratched her head as she failed to understand the overly sweet, friendly Priya today. However, out of guilt for her liking Rahul, she decided to agree to the party plan. She hoped this would stop further queries from Priya and end the topic for now, but Priya refused to give up.

"Let's have a brunch party at Rahul's flat. I will invite a few school friends and you invite Rajeev. I am sure you would want him to be comfortable with your other friends as it seems he is not going anywhere anytime soon," Priya said excitedly, already planning the party in her mind.

Nikita got a little scared with such abrupt planning as she was sure Rajeev would not appreciate being forced to meet so many strangers. She tried to explain and calm Priya, "I am not sure he will be comfortable or even want to talk to strangers much younger than him and from a completely different field. What will he talk about with them? I am not even sure if he is free as he hates wasting time on things that do not help him get more business or have some monetary benefit. Time is like money for him so he meticulously plans how he spends his day."

Priya laughed as she replied, "Really? And yet he spends the full day frivolously talking to you. I think I understand that guy more than you do. I can bet he will jump at the offer to spend another day with you. Don't worry, I will make him comfortable with our gang. My specialty is hosting parties, so don't doubt my talents. Just focus on bringing Rajeev around."

Nikita was still not convinced, but Priya impulsively hugged her and said, "Just bring him around. I want to make sure Rahul and Rajeev's problem gets solved so we can hang out without these confrontations and hide-and-seek games."

As Priya left, Nikita tried to make a half-hearted call to invite Rajeev. She still wasn't convinced she wanted to deal with another Rajeev-Rahul brawl. They were both her friends, and she didn't want to be put in a position where she had to choose between them. So, if Priya wanted to help make the situation better, Nikita decided to give it a try too.

TWENTY-ONE
THE BRUNCH BRAWL

Priya was busy with the arrangements after coaxing a reluctant Rahul to sit on the sofa, where he sat sulking. She had also convinced him not to open his mouth for the day after a long session of emotional blackmail. Nikita stood jittery at the door, looking down the hallway in anticipation of Rajeev's arrival, occasionally stealing glances at Rahul, who seemed to be having a hard time containing his anger. Rakshit and the rest of the annoying gang had arrived, and their banter was helping to distract her.

"So, what's up with this party? I mean, I get it that we all are shocked out of our minds that Nikki managed to get one guy to like her, but seriously Priya, be a little subtle about making fun of her," Rakshit taunted, slinging his arm around Nikita's shoulder.

Nikita removed his hand as she retorted, "Priya had been planning the 'meet the girlfriend' party for you for ages, but considering your track record of how many women dumped you immediately after meeting you, she didn't want to waste the party supplies and decided to use them for me."

"I didn't realize I was the guest of honor and that everyone would be waiting to greet me at the door," Rajeev remarked as he arrived, wrapping his arms around Nikita from behind and planting a possessive 'She's mine' kiss on her cheek. Rahul, visibly upset, stormed out of the hall, slamming the bedroom door behind him as he retreated to collapse on his bed. The peace he sought in his room was shattered within seconds as Priya followed him inside.

"What did we decide about overreacting and pretending to be civil? I don't think you plan on letting my brunch be peaceful," Priya stood in the doorway with her arms crossed, staring at Rahul.

Rahul closed his eyes, hoping against hope that he was in a dream, but Priya was still standing there when he opened them. He had to reply, "I am trying to make sure it is peaceful by disappearing from the venue because if I see that psycho put his hand around Nikita, I swear I will not be able to control my punch."

Priya had to literally pull Rahul and drag him to the hall where everyone had already gathered around their home theater. Rakshit was screaming at the top of his lungs to start the movie. Rahul rolled his eyes as he saw Nikita and Rajeev sitting close. Priya pushed him to sit nearby while she went to get snacks.

Rahul's anger nearly boiled over when Rakshit kept asking him about the movie. He casually threw the remote at him and said, "Pick whatever movie you like and stop bothering me." Meanwhile, Rahul's eyes kept darting toward Nikita, closely observing her every move. Noticing his disapproving glances, Nikita, feeling uncomfortable, shifted slightly away from Rajeev.

Rahul's clenched fists relaxed for a moment as he turned his attention to the movie, but this change in demeanor was noticeable, especially to Rajeev. Sensing an opportunity, Rajeev took it up a notch. He draped his arm around Nikita's shoulders and intertwined his hand with hers as they discussed the movie scene.

Unable to stand the sight any longer, Rahul got up in frustration and headed to the kitchen, ostensibly to bring more food or at least to help Priya, so he wouldn't have to watch the public display of affection anymore. "What kind of friends sit like this? Look at the guy's hands and legs. He looks like a pervert. I don't get why Nikita can't see all this," Rahul complained to Priya.

Priya, sensing the depth of Rahul's agitation and fearing her suspicions about his feelings for Nikita were coming true, tried to keep her composure. She had hoped to be wrong, but the only solace was that neither Rahul nor Nikita seemed to realize what was happening. Priya knew she had to make sure they never did.

Priya struck Rahul's head and said, "Rakshit and I have sat like this millions of times, and so have you with Nikita and other girls. Will you relax for a bit and stop spoiling the party? Nikita seems perfectly safe and sound, so please don't ruin it for everyone around with your weird theories." They both carried the remaining food and sat on the floor rugs, with Rahul still within viewing angle of Nikita and Rajeev's hand games.

Determined to return the favor, Rahul hugged Priya from behind and kissed her neck while keeping an eye on Nikita to gauge her reaction. Nikita turned towards them, smiled, and then returned her gaze to the movie. Rahul was taken aback. Her indifference to his closeness with Priya hurt him more than her closeness with Rajeev. He struggled to make sense of why she didn't get jealous. Maybe she hid her feelings well, but the calmness in her eyes told him that it wasn't true—she truly didn't care.

As Rahul's frustration mounted, his fidgeting fingers tightened around the wine glass in his hand, and it shattered under the pressure. The noise made everyone turn towards him, so Rahul left for the bathroom. He didn't want anyone's attention on him, especially now. Rahul felt someone standing in the doorway, so he murmured as he washed his hands, "Can you please leave me alone for now? I tried to be civil, but I can't be forced to see his perverted antics anymore."

"Whose?" Nikita asked, making Rahul turn in surprise. He shrugged and headed into his bedroom, replying, "Who else? Your so-called friend who thinks he is your husband, but you refuse to even acknowledge him as a boyfriend. The guy who not so long ago insulted you in that hotel. Did you recognize him, or should I keep going with my list of descriptions for him? Because it's a pretty long one."

Nikita sat on the bed and said exasperatedly, "I don't get what your problem is with him or what his problem is with you. I just, for once, want peace where my only two friends don't bitch about each other constantly."

"I don't get what your problem is, Nikki. That guy has mocked you multiple times in just the few days you've known him, and yet you still cling to him and his so-called friendship. Meanwhile, I've told you multiple times that I like you, but you keep your distance from me. If this is some lame attempt to make me jealous and make me choose between you and Priya, then all I would say is that Rajeev is taking advantage of this stupid game of yours," Rahul said as he sat down next to her.

"I am not playing games. I wish, for once, you would understand me," Nikita replied, resting her head on Rahul's shoulder and trying to hold his hand. She heard a noise at the door and saw Rajeev staring at her, then turning away in disgust as he walked off. She yanked her hand away from Rahul and ran towards the door, but Rajeev was nowhere in sight.

Rahul went after her and tried to stop Nikita. "What is wrong with you? Let him go if he's getting angry just because you talked with your friend. Can't you see how ridiculous it is, and still, you are running after him?" Nikita pushed him away. "He's upset. You don't know him. I have to talk to him before he misunderstands everything."

She ran outside, catching sight of Rajeev entering the lift. She caught hold of his hand and kept saying, "I'm sorry. Let me explain. It's not what it looked like."

Rajeev shook her off and muttered in anger, "You can be okay with being treated like a backup plan, but I don't want to get involved in this forced love triangle that this guy is creating and you're happily being a part of, at the expense of your own respect." The force made Nikita stumble and fall back as the lift doors closed.

Rahul hurried to pick her up. "How the hell can he push you like this? Who does he think he is? I'll make sure he regrets this for the rest of his life." He kept talking, but it was clear Nikita wasn't listening. She was too phased out, and then suddenly, she decided to run down the stairs.

Rahul was taken aback for a moment, unsure if he should follow her. He was jerked back into reality by the sound of the lift arriving on his floor. Deciding to go down and see how the drama would unfold, he followed. By the time he reached the ground floor, he saw Nikita leaning inside Rajeev's car, incessantly apologizing as Rajeev tried to start the engine.

Rahul pulled Nikita back as Rajeev sped off without a word, leaving her sobbing uncontrollably. Glancing at the speeding car, Rahul comforted Nikita with a gentle pat on her shoulder, his mind racing as he grappled with the sinking feeling that he had lost her for good.

TWENTY-TWO
RAHUL CONFESSES

"The whole weekend has passed, and you haven't stopped staring at your phone for even a second. What is wrong with you? Why are you behaving like a love-struck puppy who has been kicked? If he doesn't want to talk to you, don't you have other people around who are dying to talk to you? We wasted the whole weekend with your sulking, trying to help you snap out of it. He will call when he wants to. You've left him thousands of messages, so it's time to give some importance to your self-respect too," Rahul tried to get through to a sullen Nikita, constantly holding her by her shoulders and shaking her.

Nikita got irritated and shouted, "I didn't ask you to stay with me. You and Priya are not attached to me at the hip, so you can easily go out on your own, which by the way, you have done multiple times before. Why the sudden concern?"

Rahul tried to calm her by hugging her as he replied, "I want my old Nikki back. This irritated and half-depressed Nikki is ruining the aura of our flat, what say, Pri?" Nikita wrenched herself from his hug and replied irritated, "There is a flat with a completely perfect aura right opposite to this one, so please let me be at peace in this one."

Priya couldn't take this 'Rahul over-pampering Nikita' scene anymore and decided to put a stop to it. "Look, we are just worried because last time Rajeev caused your emotional break down. We don't want a repeat telecast of it. We don't want to interfere in your personal matters, but Rahul was just being cautious because of your past behavior."

Turning to Rahul, she said, "Rahul, let's go. She wants to be alone for a bit. Can we finally go out since she clearly doesn't appreciate us being around? Rakshit has called from the Friends Cafe below."

Rahul looked at Nikita, who seemed unperturbed even after Priya's long accusatory speech. "Pri, you can go meet Rakshit. I'm going to stay and finish the movie we were watching last night while keeping an eye on this dumbo Nikki. Besides, I can't stand Rakshit for more than five minutes, so stop trying to put us in same room and force us to become friends. We're not your guinea pigs that you can put in a cage to fulfill your fantasy friendship experiments."

Priya was undecided about leaving but kept getting calls from Rakshit. Realizing that Rahul was in no mood to meet him, she thought a quick downstairs visit would be better than arguing with Rahul. "Fine, I'll be back soon. Try not to kill each other," Priya said as she grabbed her bag and headed out.

With Priya out of sight, Rahul did not waste a second. He embraced and caressed Nikita again, speaking to her in a soothing voice, "Nikki, you need to understand that guy is trying reverse psychology on you. He is making himself inaccessible to you, and you, like a fool, are running after him. It's a common human tendency to want something you can't get, and he is using this to attract you. He's a womanizer who will use and throw you away in less than a day. I wish I could drill this sense into your head."

Nikita, who had been sitting and staring at the hardwood floor, finally looked up at Rahul, her eyes full of disgust. Even Rahul was taken aback for a second. "He is not doing anything. Will you stop degrading the guy who has done nothing but taken care of me? What is your problem with him? You don't like him, I got that. I like him, so get that through your head too and stop talking about him. That's the least you can do," Nikita almost screamed at him as she got up.

Rahul held her hand, gently rubbing it to calm her down as he made her sit next to him. "I don't have a problem with the guy. I guess I'm just becoming overprotective about you," he admitted. "I hate seeing you cry or even slightly sad. I hate it even more when it's because of someone else who's not me."

Rahul's words made Nikita turn and look at him in surprise. He continued, "I hate when you get so adversely affected by anyone or give more importance to someone else other than me. I know I'm being selfish when I say this, but I want to be your one and only priority, even though I'm not offering you the same. I wish I could make you understand that both you and Priya are important to me, and I want to keep these two relationships forever. I don't know what to call such relationships, and I can't give our relationship the name you want. So, the ball is in your court. Don't make me choose between you and Priya, because I need you both."

Nikita felt frustrated as she shook her head and replied, "Everything is not about you, Rahul. I liked you, and you didn't like me in that way. I'm grown-up enough to understand that and not use other guys to make you jealous. We will be friends forever. Let's end this topic once and for all. Whenever I see Priya, I feel guilty for the way I've behaved, which thankfully she has no idea about. I want it to stay that way, and I want to move on. Rajeev is helping me move on from you, and you are not. I'm not making you choose between Priya and me. You're making me choose between you and Rajeev, so let's end this conversation. Just because I'm friends with other people doesn't end my friendship with you. There, your problem is solved. Now, can I peacefully cry over Rajeev not picking up my phone?"

Rahul cupped her face between his hands and made her look at him as he said, "I don't want to be friends with you. I want to be your one and only friend. I hate you talking with any other guy. You've never given any importance to any guy until you met Rajeev. You refused to talk to all the guys who tried to take you on a date just because I didn't like them. But everything changed when Rajeev came. You won't cut ties with him even when I told you to. The way his silence affects you makes me wonder if he has become more important to you than I ever was, and I hate that. So, no, my problem is not solved because I love you, and I can't stand the thought of you with any other guy. I hope my problem is clear to you now."

Priya stood at the door, overhearing everything, and watched as Rahul kiss Nikita on her cheek. She slowly moved away and closed the door behind her as she took out her phone and dialed Rajeev's number.

TWENTY-THREE
Rajeev And Priya Team Up

Priya was getting dressed as she looked around the room in admiration. "Now I understand why Nikita keeps coming here. This room and your entire villa speak of your extravagant lifestyle, but somehow, they've failed to keep Nikita loyal to you, as she still hasn't stopped clinging to Rahul. I just don't understand how a girl like her has managed to get two affluent guys to fall head over heels for her." She paused, adjusting her dress, and then looked at Rajeev. "By the way, I know why I did what I did today, but why did you agree to do it? I thought you loved Nikita."

Rajeev got up from the bed and wrapped his robe around himself as he spoke, "Don't take this too seriously. Now, tell me about the plan you mentioned on the phone. I hope you have other ideas besides jumping on me to break them up. We both are their second priorities, so if you think this date of ours is going to cause any ripples in their love story, then you are highly mistaken."

Priya smiled as she turned towards him, holding his hand while speaking, "This was just because I was pissed off seeing both of them. But make no mistake, I am the first priority for people around me, even if they have several backup plans. I need your help to make sure Nikki knows she is a backup plan for Rahul and develops at least some self-respect so as to not continue being that backup. Otherwise, there is no way Rahul will let her go."

Rajeev sat down with a smirk on his face as he replied, "I hope I had the same confidence in your plan as you have in Rahul's love for you. I, on the other hand, have no doubts about Nikita's feelings for Rahul, and erasing him from her life is literally not possible."

Priya smiled as she spoke, "That's why I needed to know if you are ready to go to any extent to make this plan work, even if it means hurting Nikki. I was a little skeptical before coming here because I thought you were madly in love with her, but today's date made me believe that you don't mind hurting our darling Nikki. So, let's partner up and make this plan work. The only way Nikki is going to leave Rahul is if he says so, and I will make it happen by making him choose between me and her. Your job would be to ensure that once she leaves, she never comes back. We need to create enough situations where they hurt each other, pushing them to stay apart and seek solace in us instead of their toxic relationship. It will start with me emotional blackmailing Rahul, and you need to stop giving Nikki the cold shoulder so that she turns to you when Rahul pushes her away."

Rajeev and Priya shook hands after she explained her entire plan in detail, and he agreed to help with the tasks that required his corporate networking skills—the sole reason Priya had involved him. She was still hesitant to trust a stranger with her plan, but desperate times called for desperate measures—even if it meant becoming allies with a psychotic guy who had come across as quite aggressive within just a few minutes of knowing him.

Priya couldn't help but feel a little scared for Nikita if she actually got romantically involved with such a guy and faced daily abuse. However, she shrugged off the thought as she left Rajeev's house, reminding herself that no girl deserves any sympathy if she tries to steal Rahul from right under her nose.

She reached her flat to find Rahul and Nikki in each other's embrace again. Rahul pushed Nikita away when he heard Priya enter and tried to mumble a lame excuse, "She is still crying for that joker Rajeev, and my cheering her up isn't working very well. Maybe you can give it a try."

Priya came near, nudged Nikita away, and gave Rahul a peck on the lips as she replied, "I need cheering up more, so let's go to your flat." Rahul signaled her to go ahead and said he would follow as he looked at Nikita, trying to gauge her reaction.

Nikita went back to her bedroom, with Rahul following her and trying to explain his actions, "I need some time to tell Priya about our situation. She behaves erratically and territorially sometimes, and I don't want her friendship with you to get spoiled over all this. I will be back in a while. Let me talk to her. You are equally important to me, and I don't want you to start thinking something stupid about being a backup, which Rajeev has fed into your head."

Nikita shrugged her shoulders and replied with a stoic expression, "Rahul, you don't need to explain anything to me or do anything out of your comfort zone for me. I'm fine with the way things are between us. You can be with whoever you want, and we will talk whenever you want. I don't have any expectations from you. Relax and go to Priya."

Rahul hesitated for a moment but decided to leave when Nikita lay down to sleep. He thought that at least the issue of Rajeev poisoning her mind had been put to rest. Nikita watched Rahul leave and picked up her phone to message Rajeev for the hundredth time about how she missed talking to him. She saw the blue double tick indicating he had read her message. That was the only response she had been getting from him in the past few days. She smiled at the thought that at least he was listening to her rants and continued messaging him her daily woes.

Rajeev lay on the bed, reading Nikita's messages, while giving instructions over the phone. "I want to make sure the news is on all major news websites, not just gossip columns. Make sure the attack on her building happens at least half an hour after the story breaks, so it doesn't seem orchestrated—it should look like a spontaneous reaction to the news, as if people are outraged. One more thing: ensure it stops the moment I call you. I want to minimize unnecessary damage."

TWENTY-FOUR

PRIYA TAKES THE EXTREME STEP

Priya had finished the shoot and was looking around for Rahul so they could go back home together, but he was nowhere to be found. Nowadays, he had become Nikita's pick-up and drop-off driver for her office trips. Priya knew very well that it was just another way for Rahul to ensure that Nikita didn't get to meet Rajeev. She picked up her phone and typed, "Today is the day, be ready!" and sent the message to Rajeev. She booked a cab, all the while practicing the dialogues of her plan and rehearsing what she would say when she caught Rahul and Nikita back home.

Nikita was glued to her phone again and had checked for the hundredth time if any message had come. She still couldn't believe that Rajeev was reading all her messages but could not type a single word from his side. Rahul pulled her near and made her lie on the sofa with her head on his lap. He started massaging her head as he tried to calm her down, "Will you stop staring at the phone for a few minutes and talk to people who actually want to talk to you? Whenever Priya is out and I want to spend some time with you, you are busy with a phone. I could have even tolerated another human being getting more importance than me, but a blank phone with no messages or working apps is taking my place, which is a little hard to digest."

"No one is more important than you, Rahul. How many times do I have to tell you that? I just don't like anyone being angry with me, so I was messaging him. Look, I will put down my phone and give you my full attention now. FYI, Priya might come back soon, so be ready to jump off the sofa," Nikita said, intertwining her fingers with Rahul's.

Rahul got offended and replied, "I'm not scared of her. I just need time to smooth out the relationship, especially when it involves you. She might have been okay with my affections towards a stranger, but she knows how close you are to me, so it will take her time to adjust to our news."

Nikita got up, saying, "There is no news, Rahul, until Priya is okay." Rahul held her hand and pulled her towards him, using both his hands to hold her face as he said, "There is news that I love you, which will not change even if Priya is okay with it or not."

A loud "What?" from the door made both of them turn towards a glaring Priya at the entrance. "Is this a joke, Rahul? Are you seriously dumping me for a classless nobody who can barely fit in her dress? You are choosing her over me? This is so embarrassing," Priya shouted at Rahul as she moved towards the kitchen. She kept rambling as she searched for something, "I can't even imagine the trolls and the media tabloids who will start comparing both of us and splash this news all across in various sorts of sarcastic ways. I will be the laughing stock of the town that even a girl like her can replace me."

She stopped as she found what she was searching for and picked it up to look at it properly—a razor-sharp chef's knife. Rahul and Nikita were gripped by fear and rushed towards Priya as Rahul mumbled an apology, "I am not leaving you. Nikita gave me an ultimatum to choose between you or her, and I got confused as she was constantly flirting with Rajeev to get my attention."

"Don't even bother with an explanation and don't even think about coming close. I just can't deal with the embarrassment this will cause," Priya said, her voice trembling. Before they could react, she slashed her wrist with the knife. Blood spurted from the wound, and she collapsed to the floor.

Rahul barely had time to reach her side. Nikita stood frozen, staring at the blood, while Rahul shouted at her to call an ambulance. He finally picked up his phone from the sofa and shook Nikita back to consciousness. "Will you do something? Go hold her hand. Hello, yeah, we need an ambulance at..." he narrated the address urgently over the phone.

Nikita bent down to hold Priya, trying to stop the bleeding. Priya pushed her hands away and whispered, "I will never forgive you."

Rahul returned to find Nikita still staring at Priya, her shock paralyzing her into inaction. His frustration boiled over, and he shouted, "What is wrong with you, Nikki? Are you waiting for her to die? You're not even bothering to help her or me. You know what? This is all your fault. I don't even want to talk to you right now. I'm taking her to the hospital. You can stay here and wait for her death instead of glaring at her while she bleeds."

With that, he lifted Priya in his arms and ran out of the flat. As he reached the parking lot, he realized he had forgotten his car keys and cursed loudly. Turning back to go upstairs, he saw Nikita standing right behind him. She handed him the keys and said, "I was just in shock for a second. Why would I want anything to happen to her? How could you even think such a thing about me?"

"Can you stop this attention-seeking drama for now? With your due permission, can I give importance to Pri for a few minutes?" Rahul cut her short, started the car, and drove off to the hospital.

Nikita dialed Rajeev's number, tears streaming down her cheeks, but there was no answer. She sent a message, briefly explaining the incident and begging him to call back soon. She kept waiting for the call, pacing up and down her flat. When daylight started to filter through the curtains, she realized she had fallen asleep on the floor carpet.

She picked up her phone and felt a sickening realization—it had been hours since the incident, and neither Rahul nor Rajeev had called her back. Determined to go to the hospital, she took a step toward her bedroom, but a crackling sound interrupted her. A stone landed at her feet, shattering her window. She moved towards the gaping hole, only for a few more stones to be thrown inside.

Nikita took refuge behind her sofa, hoping the stone pelting would cease. The doorbell rang, startling her into almost screaming. Fear paralyzed her, but then she heard Rajeev's voice, urging her to open the door. Determined, she crawled towards the door, a slow, painstaking journey that took nearly ten minutes as the stones continued to rain down. Finally, she managed to open the door and pulled a surprised Rajeev inside, dragging him to the safety of her sofa's shelter.

"I don't know what is happening, but you need to lie low, or a stone is going to pop open your head," Nikita said, covering his head and forcing him down behind the sofa. "You didn't see the news. That's why I am here," Rajeev replied, surprise evident in his eyes. Nikita, still confused and weary from the previous night's ordeal, responded, "I don't know. I didn't check my phone. What happened?"

TWENTY-FIVE

NIKITA MOVES IN WITH RAJEEV

Rajeev gently led a visibly shaken Nikita to her bedroom, offering her a glass of water as he explained the situation. "Priya's news is all over the tabloids. Her fans, and I guess your Rahul's fans, are calling you a homewrecker. They gathered around the building to protest, but some idiots decided stone throwing would be a better sport. I didn't know the situation was this bad until I reached the building, so I called the police. Hopefully, they will disperse the crowd soon. Don't worry."

The cacophony outside showed no sign of diminishing. Nikita, overwhelmed, slumped onto the bed, covering her ears with pillows, desperately wishing it were all a nightmare. Her thoughts raced as she struggled to process the events of the past few hours.

Rajeev stayed by Nikita's side, his hand gently caressing her hair, attempting to soothe her. "You can shift to my house for a while until this fan mania dies down. I didn't know those two wannabes had any fans. The increasing number of unemployed youths in this country is frightening." His attempt at humor fell flat as he heard her soft sobbing from under the pillows.

He began patting her back, and suddenly, Nikita got up and hugged him, crying incessantly. Rajeev continued to pat her back, trying to calm her down. It was only when the crowd noise outside finally stopped that Nikita began to compose herself. She pulled away from the embrace, wiping her tears, and asked frantically, "Did the police come? What happened? Are all of them arrested?" Before Rajeev could answer, Nikita hurried to the window. He followed, trying to stop her, but she was determined.

As they both stared at the empty streets from the window, Rajeev held Nikita's shoulder and said, "There is no guarantee that they won't return, so you need to move out from here." "I can't. Rahul may come back or need some help. I don't even know what is happening there. He keeps cutting my calls. What if he calls and needs anything? I have to stay here," Nikita was still mumbling as she fiddled with her fingers.

Rajeev held her hand firmly and said, "Are you serious? He hasn't called, and he is not going to call. Anyway, I am not wasting any more time here explaining what a douche bag Rahul is. But just in case he calls and needs anything, I assure you, I will take you to him immediately. My house is stocked with everything that your Rahul may need, so just stop thinking about them for a while and start thinking about yourself for once. This place is not safe, and I am not leaving you alone here."

Rajeev went to her bedroom and started pulling out her stuff to pack in her bag while she frantically kept dialing Rahul and Priya's numbers with no success. When they got to the parking lot with her bags, she gave the keys to the guard and told him about the broken window, "Get it fixed and give the keys to Rahul when he comes. I will be gone for a while, some personal issue." The guard gave quizzical glances to the keys and also her but finally nodded.

Nikita got into Rajeev's car; her anxiety still evident. "So, what did the news say about me and this situation? You said you read the news and came. Which one? You only watch those boring business news channels. I hope they were not showing these things about me." As she looked at him sheepishly, Rajeev pulled her cheeks gently and replied, "Some news shorts that keep sending useless notifications and are mostly entertainment channels. It's better you stay away from news also for a bit till Priya recovers."

"Can we go to the hospital? I just need to look at her once. Then we will go wherever you say," Nikita looked at him with pleading eyes. He agreed, but all the while he was driving the car, he kept searching his brain for a good reason to escape this situation. However he could come up with nothing. When they reached the hospital, with Rajeev's help, it took no time to locate Priya's room, especially with Rahul pacing outside it in frustration.

His frustration turned to confusion when he saw Nikita, and then to extreme anger when he saw Rajeev and his hand around Nikita's waist. "What do you think you are doing here? Have you come to enjoy the climax of the drama you created or to create more with this joker of yours? Unfortunately, she is still alive, so I don't think you will be able to party yet," Rahul said with a smirk.

Nikita could barely speak as she felt choked with emotions. "How can you even think I would want her to die? No one believes me. Even your fans attacked my flat in the morning. Do you have any idea what they did? I kept calling you."

"Nikki, please. For once, stop your narcissistic behavior. I don't want to hear about your problems when Priya is dying in the other room. You just couldn't let things be. You have to have everything. You started this jealousy game with Rajeev to get my attention. Then you created more drama about making me choose between you and Pri. Now you brought him here to give the final touches to your plan of ruining everyone's life. You just couldn't let anyone be happy. What Pri did is your fault, and if anything happens to her, I will never forgive you. Just get out of my face. If you stand here even for a second more, I will forget we are in a hospital," Rahul said with clenched fists and menacing eyes.

Nikita turned and dashed out of there, with Rajeev calling her back. Rahul shook his head, but as he turned to leave too, Rajeev caught his shoulder and, with a smirk on his face, said, "Thanks!"

Rajeev was half expecting to offer his shoulder to a hysterical Nikita, but instead, he found her standing near the car, looking determined to punch anyone who came near her.

"He started everything," she blurted out while pacing near the car. "He came on to me when Priya caught us. I told him we shouldn't do anything because Priya looked uncomfortable. But the last few days, while you were not replying to my messages, he spent full days at my flat, totally ignoring Priya and pretending to care for me. He spent days talking to me and avoiding her, but now he's putting all the blame on me for Priya's actions. He's unbelievable. He's so spineless that he was scared to tell Priya that he liked me, and now he doesn't have the courage to even accept to himself that this happened because of him."

Rajeev held her by the waist and tried to make her get in the car. "Fine, let's have this discussion in the car as I don't trust any place to be devoid of their moronic fans." Once they were back on the road, Rajeev looked in her direction, smiling. "I must say I am a little surprised. I thought you would be emotional that Rahul treated you that way. However, I like this way of getting upset."

Nikita replied, "I am not upset, just a bit angry that for the last few days, he was hounding me, and then he had the audacity to put all the blame on me. I didn't even say I loved him or had any intention of making him jealous. I was so upset that you weren't talking to me, and he started his love drama on the side." Rajeev kept stealing happy glances in Nikita's direction until they reached his house.

"So, this is my room, and there are a few other rooms across the hall that you can choose from. There's one for Philip, who you know from the office, and another for my domestic help. Leaving those two, the rest of the house is open for your selection," Rajeev said, showing her around the house. He stopped in his tracks as she replied, "Why can't I sleep in the same room as you? The bed is big enough to fit two, and I'm too scared to stay alone for a while. I mean, if you don't have any problem, of course."

Rajeev was too surprised to utter any words and just managed to shake his head while Nikita proceeded to find space for all her stuff. "I don't have much, do I? I literally walked out of that toxic so-called relationship in a few minutes with just two bags. I have no idea what took me so long. I just hope she gets well soon so that I can get rid of the one last guilt I have for them," Nikita said as she put her clothes in the cupboard.

"One good sign was that she wasn't in the ICU but in a normal private room, so maybe the cut wasn't too deep and she's out of danger. Anyway, they were your only friends since childhood. It will be difficult to cut them off so soon," Rajeev said as he lay down on the bed. Nikita came and lay down beside him, replying, "They were the ones who blamed me for everything wrong in their lives, and they ensured I had no other friends, so I don't think the cut-off will be that difficult."

They looked at each other, and then Rajeev extended his arms, signaling her to come closer. While the two slept peacefully in each other's arms, Rahul's string of bad news seemed to have no end. Despite the operation being successful, the doctor remained skeptical of Priya's recovery, as she had not yet regained consciousness.

TWENTY-SIX

THE MUDSLINGING STARTS

It was almost a week before the doctor finally allowed Priya to leave the hospital. Although she recovered quickly from her physical wounds, they kept her for a few days to monitor her for depression or any other emotional health-related issues. Her parents had arrived, but Priya insisted on going back to her flat with Rahul, stating he had not left her side since last week.

As soon as the car reached their building, the guard came running and handed them the keys that Nikita had left behind, saying, "I have got the windows fixed as Madam had asked. She told me to give the keys whenever you returned."

Priya asked a puzzled Rahul, "Did you make her leave just for me?" and hugged him in excitement. Rahul was still confused but patted her back instead of confessing the truth, as he didn't want to say anything to upset her at the moment.

After tucking Priya in bed and placing a glass of water by her side, Rahul said, "I'll check the flat to see if everything is alright. The watchman mentioned a broken window. I'll be back soon." Priya opened her mouth to protest but then reconsidered, realizing Nikita might not be there. She decided to settle back and take a nap instead, as she felt tired.

Rahul called the guard up and opened Nikita's flat to inspect the damages. As the guard arrived, Rahul tried to give him some money for the window repair, but the guard refused, saying, "Nikita Madam already gave me, sir. She just told me to repair everything and give you the keys."

Rahul walked around the flat with the guard, pointing out the damages and asking for details. "I don't know, sir. A few random people came, threw stones for some time, and then left before the police arrived. I didn't understand it, but Rajeev sir had told me to call the police, so I did," the guard explained.

"When did Rajeev Sir come?" Rahul was intrigued, as he hadn't told anyone about what happened with Priya, and the hospital staff, who knew him for years, would never leak news like this.

"Sir, he thankfully appeared a few minutes after the first stone was thrown," the guard replied. After a few more queries, Rahul let the guard go but remained unsure of how the fans and tabloids got the information.

Even if Nikita had called Rajeev, there was no way she would leak the news to the press. He kept pacing the floor, suspecting that Nikita might have leaked the information and created the drama to garner sympathy. He thought she might have made one last attempt to get his attention by coming to the hospital and pretending to care about Priya.

He struggled to convince himself that Nikita was not to be trusted, but he just couldn't believe that his Nikki could do something like this. He needed to confront her for his personal sanity, as the incidents just didn't add up in his head.

When he returned to check on Priya, she was sound asleep. He made the impromptu decision to find Nikita. He tried calling her, but the calls didn't go through. He decided to make a stop at the most obvious place. "So, Rajeev has a bungalow; is that why she refused to cut off ties with him even after..." Rahul's thoughts were interrupted when the guards asked him whom he wanted to meet.

Rajeev picked up the house phone and looked at Nikita as he said, "Do you want to see Rahul?" Nikita was surprised but nodded, thinking he might have some news about Priya. Rajeev told his guard to let Rahul in, all the while staring at Nikita, who was nervously fiddling with her fingers again. "How is Priya?" Nikita asked as soon as she saw Rahul entering the hall.

"Are you done with your drama and jealousy game? I didn't think you would stoop so low that you would make people throw stones at our flat. And which news channel did you leak stories to? I was a bit surprised at the move, but I guess a person who is using her own friend's suicide attempt for her selfish needs can find ways to do anything. Anyways, I don't want to wash our dirty linen in front of this guy, so let's go back and we can talk."

Nikita was too shocked to utter a word after all the allegations and kept staring at Rahul. Rahul's irritation level was rising with Nikita not saying anything and Rajeev staring at them with his usual smirk. Rahul came near Nikita and pulled her hand, saying, "I don't want to do this drama in front of randoms. Let's go." Nikita brushed off his hand immediately and stared at him in shock.

She finally gathered her breath and managed to speak, "I didn't do any of those things you mentioned, but if you can think like that about me after staying with me for years, then I don't want to give any other explanation. I am not coming back to your flat. Priya is clearly not okay with me, and I don't want to aggravate her emotional turmoil any more as I have seen enough blood for a lifetime. I don't want to blame Priya for her misunderstandings, as you have even worse ones about me, so it is better I stay out of your lives. Trust me, no one would be happier than me if you two get married."

Rahul was not ready to give up yet and raised his voice, "I don't get what game you are playing, but I really don't want to have this discussion here. I am not going to say it again, Nikki. We need to leave from here right now."

Nikita shook her head and shifted behind Rajeev. "I am done with my life splashed all over newspapers and my family being abused due to my behavior. I am ruining everyone's lives by being near you, so this needs to end here."

Rahul did not wait for her to finish and stormed off. He still could not figure out Nikita's contacts with news reporters, but considering the influential Rajeev, anything was possible. By the time he reached home, Priya was already up and looking at him with quizzical eyes, so he made up a story, "I had forgotten to buy some medicines, so I had gone out but couldn't find them. I will order online. How are you feeling?" He hugged her and took her back to bed for rest.

"Hey, what are you thinking?" Priya said while running her fingers through his hair. Rahul sat down near her, saying, "Nothing much. I need to go file a case on the people who attacked our flat. I still don't get how they knew it was where Nikita lives, as she is not a celebrity. Did they just assume that she lives with me? I also don't understand who are these fans obsessed with us when we have not even publicly said that we are dating. Lots of questions but no answers. So anyway, the first step is to report to the police."

Priya held his hand as he got up to leave, "What's the need? Nikki is not living here anymore, and the windows are repaired, so no damage was caused. Just stay with me. I don't want to spend even a minute apart from you now that Nikki is out of our lives for good." Rahul looked at her in surprise as he sat down again.

It was a while before Rahul spoke. "I have an idea. Let's do an Insta live together and tell everyone that you are safe and healthy so they don't attack my house again," Rahul said, smiling as he played with her hair. Priya sat up and gave him a skeptical gaze, "It would mean that we acknowledge we are together and even living together."

"Yes, why not? You love me, right? That's why you cut your hand. I want to show everyone how much you love me. Come on, get dressed and come out to the living room," Rahul got up, excited by his idea. He had already set up the room and his phone camera for their live on Insta by the time Priya entered the living room. He pulled her close as she sat down and then started the live.

"Hey friends, how are you all? This is a small impromptu Hi just to say thanks to both our fans. Priya has now fully recovered from a small surgery, but hopefully she never recovers from her love obsession for me," Rahul smiled and looked at Priya, expecting her to speak. When she didn't respond, he continued with his speech. "We know you all are very protective of us, but damaging my flat because of Nikita is not cool. Let her be. She was a gold digger who has moved on with her life to another sugar daddy of hers. We wish her all the luck and want our fans to forgive and forget her like we have. She has done something..."

Priya watched in surprise as Rahul went on and on, ranting about Nikita and her character. She realized that the interaction with fans was not to declare their relationship but to use this opportunity to bash Nikita. She tried to control her anger in front of the live audience, but it was difficult to digest that even hatred for Nikita held more importance in Rahul's life than love for her. She had long lost to Nikita but was still struggling to accept this loss.

After finishing the Nikita roasting session, Rahul finally acknowledged Priya's existence on the same sofa and turned to give her an elated, kiddish smile. It was as if he had won some competition in school and was showing the trophy to his family. "This is how you make news. Nikki won't know what hit her when all the news channels run with this gossip—'Rahul calls Nikita a gold digger!' It will be fun to watch. Let's wait for some time."

Priya lay down on the sofa in exhaustion and questioned, "Why don't you think that they will run the headlines about our relationship becoming official? I thought that's what the Insta live was all about, so that should be the main news. Isn't it?"

Rahul was caught off guard but managed a smile. "Of course, it will be all about us." Priya sighed and tried to sleep as Rahul patted her back with one hand and kept scrolling his phone with the other to check on the news updates.

Nikita was lying on Rajeev's lap, sharing her office issues with him while he navigated through the news channels. Nothing captured his attention until one reporter said, "Music sensation Rahul calls his close friend and model Nikita a gold digger." Nikita turned around while Rajeev made a face and quickly changed the channel. She took the remote from him and went back to the same channel, where they were describing the entire Insta live session of Rahul and calling him savage for roasting a gold digger like Nikita.

"What is wrong with him? What money did I take? I worked for his production and was paid my due amount. I didn't even want to stay in his flat. They both forced me to stay, saying I could pay them the same rent as I would have paid for some other flat. He is so petty," Nikita fumed as she paced up and down in anger.

Rajeev switched off the TV and said, "I thought you had closed the Rahul chapter, but it looks like he wants attention every day and you like giving it to him." Nikita looked at him in surprise. "If I don't tell my side, then everyone will think whatever he said is true. It makes me look guilty."

"How about you completely ignore him and pretend you never heard what he said because he doesn't matter, as you have already proclaimed before? Prove yourself right and deny him the attention he seeks. Seems like a better plan than yours. What do you say?" Rajeev held her shoulders and made her sit as he tried to calm her down.

Nikita crossed her legs as she sat and grumbled, "I am not a gold digger. I can also say many things about them, like a few secrets that would be damaging for their reputations, but I don't want to stoop to his level, and he does not matter to me at all."

Rajeev was intrigued and asked, "What secrets?" but Nikita just rested her head on his shoulders, saying, "Nothing important."

TWENTY-SEVEN

THE PROPOSAL BRINGS OUT THE HAUNTING STORY

Rajeev had hoped the news would die down in a few days, but more than two weeks had passed, and he had run out of excuses to hide Nikita's phone and TV remote. Nikita understood why she was being kept away from all kinds of media, but she had stuck to her stand of not retaliating and pretending Rahul didn't matter. It was becoming increasingly difficult for her to maintain this facade, as she hadn't talked to Rahul in the longest time and he still mattered to her. However, she knew Rajeev would be hurt if she went back to Rahul now.

She smiled, thinking about how protective Rajeev was of her and how he got angrier for her well-being than she did. "You can't keep guarding the TV forever. Rahul is not going to stop," Nikita said with a smile as she hugged Rajeev. "When he decides to put people down, he goes all out. You need to stop worrying about me. I'm a big girl."

Rajeev comforted her, patting her back. "Rahul is just trying to get attention. For the first time, you've refused to follow his instructions, and his ego is hurt. He won't stop until he makes you squirm and retaliate. Ignoring him is what he can't handle. If you acknowledge his poking, he will jump to respond. It's better to stay away from the media for a while."

Nikita made a sulky face. "How long? I've taken so many work-from-home days that the office might think I'm better off staying home. What if I become irrelevant to them and they fire me?" Rajeev smiled, placing his hands on her shoulders. "Then I'll hire you back."

Nikita shrugged off his hand and said, "Please be serious. I am going to the office, and in the evening, I have to look for a few houses that have put up ads for rent. I will be late today." Rajeev was taken aback. "What rent? What houses?"

"I can't keep living here. I think the issue of their fans attacking me is solved since Priya is doing fine, and I don't want to keep living off guys and listening to the gold-digger tag anymore." Nikita replied in frustration.

Rajeev tried to control his anger with a smirk. "It is unbelievable how that guy has such control over you that with a few words he can make you do whatever he wants. You stop thinking for yourself and keep thinking of ways to please Rahul. Your Rahul obsession will not let you live your life on your terms as you have no personal opinion or any stand for yourself. Only the likes and dislikes of Rahul decide what step you would take next."

Nikita came near and cupped his face with both her hands, saying, "I don't care what anyone thinks, but I don't want to keep depending on others for a house. If I keep taking favors, I feel indebted to them. I want you and me to be with each other because we like each other's company and not because I feel I have to return a favor or something. I need a house of my own so that I have less dependency on others. I would feel less guilty if we were dating or married, but I can't overstay my welcome by encashing on a favor of a friend. I have to go now. I will see you in the evening."

"Marriage is a completely irrelevant concept for me, but if that helps to keep you here, then we can get married." Nikita was on her way out, but as soon as she heard this from Rajeev, she turned around in shock. After a minute, she started laughing uncontrollably, "I have never heard such a terrible proposal in my life."

Rajeev smiled as she came near and said, "You don't have to live alone and you don't have to take it as a favor. I like spending time with you, and if marriage would keep you in this house, I want to do that.I've never felt emotionally attached to anyone before, but with you, I just feel this need to protect you—even after trying for months to cut you off. If you are in front of my eyes, I would be at peace, so stay here and we will get a marriage certificate so that you don't feel guilty living in my house."

The smile left Nikita's face as she replied, "I like staying here, but you don't have to marry me. You don't know anything about me. I am not a good person. You don't know my past."

Rajeev, who had her full bio-data researched by Philip, was still intrigued by her words. "So, tell me then, what past stories should I know about? I will drive you to the office and we can talk on the way."

Nikita was taken aback by his upfront queries and searched her head for some excuse, but Rajeev had already started dragging her to his parking area by pulling her by the elbow. She could only manage a meek, "It's a long story." Rajeev replied, "Then you better start fast as your office is not that far away."

"I can't tell you. It was something kind of illegal," Nikita said, fiddling with her hands in nervousness. Rajeev was intrigued and asked, "You think I will hand you over to the police for something you did in your past? Thanks for this level of trust in me."

Nikita smiled. "No, it was not just me but a few others. I don't want to implicate my friends. I also don't want you to rush into any relationship with me thinking I'm some 'miss goody two shoes.'"

Rajeev parked the car at the side of the road, looked at her, and smiled. "I never thought you were that, but now you have seriously got my attention. I thought I knew everything about you since you have not stopped blabbering about your school, college, and Bollywood journey stories. So what did I miss? What crime have you committed? I want something big like theft or murder. Please don't tell me you tweeted something that hurt political or religious sentiments."

Nikita turned and hugged him as she said, "What if you hate me after the big reveal?" He patted her, saying, "Not even a chance. Besides, I can't imagine anything you've done could be worse than the things I did in my youth, especially my teenage years. Look, you tell me what you did, and I'll tell you something bad that I did. Deal?"

Nikita smiled and said, "It was in school when we all had become friends, and I had done some work for Rahul's music videos. I got the misconception that I was famous and had a huge fan following. Well, mainly a certain specific male fan following. So, long story short, there was a guy who was the top student in our class and my nemesis. But he attempted a lot of stalking to get my attention, and his coaxing, combined with my attraction to intelligence, worked. I ended up being his girlfriend. Can you drive now? I'm getting late."

Rajeev made a face and started the car while Nikita continued, "Rahul had started the 'don't trust any guy' drama, and I was trying to be rebellious, thinking some guy actually liked me and no one could tell me what to do. However, not even one date passed before he started pushing to hang out with all my friends. He would be asking about Priya and her likes and dislikes. I introduced him to Priya and Rahul, and then his true colors showed. He was obsessed with Priya and tried to find ways for us to go on double dates so he could spend the whole day talking to her. Anyways, there was nothing to break off, but to salvage my tiny self-respect, I left him. However, he continued to hover around Priya."

"You know Rahul, Priya, and their pranks, right? Well, they pulled one prank over him too, saying they were doing it to take revenge for me and then went on to humiliate him in front of the entire school. That guy went completely heartbroken and lost interest in studies. The big bad Boards came, and he failed. I guess for a consistent topper, it was too much of an insult to take, and we heard he ended his life the very next day after results came."

Rajeev looked at her quizzically. "Okay, so someone took his life. How is this illegal for you? No one can arrest you for abetment of suicide in this case." Nikita shrugged her shoulders. "It is abetment if the guy mentioned in his last email that the reason for his suicide was humiliation caused by us." Rajeev whistled. "So, how did you manage to get out of that? Clearly, none of you went to jail."

Nikita looked down, fumbling with her hands as she replied, "He was quite obsessed with Priya, and she led him on too. He confided everything to her, so it wasn't difficult to access his emails and delete everything. Everyone blamed it on the board results. His parents were too devastated to question anything, and I guess Rahul and Priya's influential parents helped to close the case faster than usual. I could have told that guy that Priya was pranking him. I could have told his parents the truth. I could have done a lot of things in retrospect, but I guess I was angry at him and wanted my own revenge. One thing I didn't even tell Rahul was that I was actually happy that Priya was distracting him from his studies. Guess who became the topper of the boards when the main guy failed? It was me!"

The car screeched to a stop near her office, and as Nikita got down, she said, "So, you know I'm not that innocent. I knew what was happening with that guy, and I let it happen. Not only because I wanted revenge for my so-called dating fiasco, but also because I wanted to win a stupid rat race. You need to think before you start throwing proposals around."

Before the car door completely closed, Rajeev shouted, "The proposal stands and the ball is in your court," and sped away.

TWENTY-EIGHT

THE WEDDING PLANNING BEGINS

"It's been a week and you didn't ask me the answer to your marriage question," Nikita snuck up behind Rajeev as he was watering the plants in the morning. Rajeev replied without turning, "I know the answer, so I didn't ask. You are free to decide when and where. I prefer low key though. Normal signing of documents in a court works fine for me."

Nikita placed her hand on her waist and made a face, saying, "This overconfidence is a little offensive. However, I just want to talk to Rahul once before we do anything." This finally made Rajeev turn and roll his eyes as he said, "Sure, please take Rahul's permission for our marriage. Do whatever you want. It feels like I'm in a side relationship with this Rahul."

Nikita looked down while Rajeev left in anger, but she took out her phone as soon as he was out of sight and typed, "Can we talk?" She paused for a minute but then finally hit the send button to Rahul. As soon as she got an "OK" reply from him, she eagerly dialed his number.

"What? If you want to talk with Priya and me, then you need to come here. I am not entering that guy's house ever again," Rahul's voice sounded grumpy and irritated. Nikita ignored his tone and replied, "I am marrying Rajeev. He said it is totally my wish—when, where, how, and all—but I want to do it as soon as possible. I just wanted to tell you before you heard from any media houses. Hellooo? Did you hear what I said?"

After nearly a minute, Rahul broke the silence. "Congrats on being so desperate for marriage that you marry the first guy who looks at you. Are you this jealous of me and Priya that you're ready to marry such a psychotic guy just to hurt me? I've seen the guy literally push you and verbally abuse you left, right, and center, but you're just dying to get into bed with him only to piss me off."

Nikita controlled her anger and tried to reply calmly, "Everything is not about you, Rahul. I've told you millions of times that I don't want to get between you two, but hopefully, this marriage will prove that. It was just an FYI before you heard it from a third person because even if you think I'm a pathetic person, I still respect you for all that you've done for me." "Yeah, I can see that clearly," Rahul cut the call after dissing her out.

Nikita marched inside in search of Rajeev and found him fiddling with the TV remote. She stood in front of the TV and declared, "We are getting married next week. I'll call my parents, and you can call yours. We can have a simple court marriage. I don't have any friends or siblings, and I don't talk to my relatives. What about yours?"

Rajeev got up and shrugged his shoulders. "Same here. I don't have any friends or relatives either. We can marry whenever your parents can come here. I should have let you talk to Rahul earlier. He made our marriage plan speedier." Nikita mumbled "hmm" and went to make calls.

The next morning, Rajeev woke up to find Nikita staring at him. "Ok, you are kind of scaring me in the morning," he said, trying to lighten the mood. Nikita didn't stop staring as she asked, "Who is in your family? I just realized I don't know anything about your family. I have never met them and you never even talk about them except your mom. What about your Dad? Where are your other relatives?"

Rajeev tried to sit up to reply, but Nikita had kept her hands firmly on his shoulders during her interrogation. He said meekly, "There is nothing to tell. Mom died when I was a kid. Dad sold everything, remarried, and shifted to the USA with the remaining few of my relatives. I stayed in hostels until I completed college and got a job. This house was actually one of the few things that Mom left in my name which Dad couldn't touch, so it came to me when I stopped being a minor. There, my life in a nutshell. Can I get up now and go to the bathroom peacefully?"

Nikita moved over to let him get up but didn't stop her questions, "So there is no one close to you that you want at the wedding? Do you hate your dad so much that you don't even want to send him an invite?"

Rajeev turned on his way to the bathroom and said, "I don't hate a person who is non-existent for me. Philip is the closest thing I have to a family, as he has been with me since the day I was born, so he will be there from my side for the wedding. I guess I can inform my grandmother who lives with Dad, but I don't think she can travel all the way from the USA. So, it's just me and Philip on your guest list."

Nikita came to the door and kept talking to Rajeev inside, "It's good if this is low-key. After the disastrous news that the media printed about Priya's suicide attempt and me being the villain, along with the fake stories thrown around, it really troubled my parents. Actually, it troubled their neighbors and relatives who, in turn, came and troubled my parents. So, I just don't want to attract media scrutiny to this wedding and ruin our life." Rajeev mumbled a few 'hmms' from inside the bathroom, in vague agreement with Nikita's rant."

When Rajeev came out of the washroom, he found Nikita standing on the bed with her hands on her hips, ready to fire up again. He asked, "What now? Is any part of my past life still pending to be scrutinized?"

Nikita nodded and asked, "You are way beyond the normal marriageable age in India but still single, which made me think that you are commitment-phobic. However, you hardly know me, and we haven't even gone on a proper date, but you are ready to marry me. It sounds all too fishy to me. If you didn't believe in marriage until now, then why such a hasty decision for me?"

Rajeev let out a sigh as he lay down on the bed again, "I have told you multiple times. I like spending time with you and want you to be around me, but I feel that you would be more comfortable with me if there was a publicly declared relationship between us. I don't believe in marriage, but I have seen how important it is for you, so I want to give you that."

Nikita lay down beside him and poked his cheeks as she asked, "Very romantic confession, but what if I file some fake case on you for divorce and take half your money in alimony? Don't you want me to sign some prenup to save all your money?"

Rajeev turned towards her to reply, "Interesting thought from someone who refuses to let me buy her even a single

Starbucks coffee and refuses to go to any 5-star restaurant because she can't afford to go Dutch there. Anyway, I have a standard contract document that I make all my girlfriends sign before we start any relationship, so you can sign that too." Rajeev bit his tongue as soon as he realized the unnecessary information he shared by mistake.

Nikita got up and stared at him incredulously, "What contract and what girlfriends, that too in plural? How many have you had? See, I know nothing about you, and we are getting married."

Rajeev held her by the shoulders as he saw her anger rising, "Will you please relax? There were very few and long ago. With the rise of fake rape cases most girls file on the pretext of marriage promises, I had drafted a consent form before starting a relationship just to avoid any legal hassles. That's it. Anyway, you need not sign it as it was not related to married life. Our situation is completely different."

Nikita impulsively hugged him saying, "I am a little possessive. I don't like sharing things, so I can't imagine you with anyone else. I will try to tone down my possessive reactions."

Rajeev got up and said, "Have I ever stopped you from doing anything? Just focus on the wedding planning and honeymoon destinations. Philip will help you out with the logistics, just tell him what you want. Forget about everything else."

TWENTY-NINE
RAHUL REFUSES TO MOVE ON

"I am sorry for all this paparazzi. I thought people would have forgotten me and the few minute roles that I did in childhood. Although, I think it is all because of that Rahul and his new album, which he has specifically made to put me down," Nikita told Rajeev as they waited for their car outside the airport. They were surrounded by reporters, cameras flashing nonstop.

Rajeev told Philip to start driving as they got inside the car before any more photographers came near them, "It's ok. I like a famous wife, plus I am looking good with all my tan from Australia."

Nikita smiled at him as she said, "I don't know how you always manage to uplift my mood, but I still feel like holding Rahul by his neck and dunking his full head inside an aquarium full of piranhas. He specifically chose a model that looks similar to me for his new music video and then wrote an abusive song about me. He is behaving as if I dumped him. We were not even dating!"

Rajeev caressed her shoulders to calm her as she literally shouted out her last sentence. "Don't let him get to you, Nikita. He's just trying to get a reaction out of you. Focus on us and the amazing time we had in Australia. Let's not let him ruin that."

"I know, I know. He wants a reaction out of me. These paparazzi are also following us for that. I just feel like punching him sometimes. He didn't want to date me, and now he is portraying me as a gold-digger who left him for you, a much richer guy. When did I take any money from him or you? I'm sorry. You are getting dragged into all this because of me," Nikita vented as she tried to sleep in Rajeev's lap in the back of the car.

Rajeev patted her head and said, "I have no problem except my wife is spending the full day talking about everything else but me." Nikita opened her eyes in surprise and got up to hug him, saying, "I love you. No more talks about irrelevant people."

Meanwhile, Rahul was busy showing Priya the overwhelming response he was receiving for his new song. "Just look, people love when the true face of some gold diggers are exposed. The views are coming in millions and just look at those comments on her. I didn't even have to mention her name. Everyone knows what she did and why she did."

Priya looked at him with quizzical eyes, "There are nearly seven songs in this album. Are they all about Nikki? In a few days, who composed so many songs for Nikki?"

Rahul's smile left his face as he replied, "These are not composed for Nikki. These are my feelings and thoughts about life in general when you are betrayed, and Nikki has a small part in it. I have come up with my album after so long and your one and only comment about it is that it's Nikki related? Seriously?"

Priya got up to leave and turned to reply, "I agree. You came out with this album after so long, and surprisingly it is all about what Nikki did to you a few days ago. By the way, what did she do to you? She went out of our life for good after trying to break us up. It called for a happy ending celebration, but here we are composing sad betrayal songs about it. Is it my turn to say, seriously?"

Rahul let out a quiet grumble but said nothing. He waited silently for her to leave the flat, then picked up the phone and called his manager. "Just tell the director that in the next video I want subtle references with Nikita's old modeling photos in the background so that it does not look too obvious but still conveys the message of the song. Also, tell that reporter my interview should air at prime time today. I will post the links on my social media to make sure we have enough engagement for the interview today. Everyone should talk about it."

Priya came back to the flat and said, "I am recovering well now and you have had a good response to your song. Why don't we invite a few friends over for a small celebration? I'm so bored of hearing about Nikita all day. Before you give any lame explanation, I will invite her too and want to see with my own eyes if you both are over each other or not. I don't think you would have a problem as you really didn't care much about her earlier, right? The songs are not ballads written for her, right? You are not that obsessed with her that you literally created an entire album on your heartbreak, right?"

Rahul shrugged his shoulders and replied, "It is your party. You can invite whoever you want. I can't keep proving my loyalty every day, especially when we are in a 'no strings attached' relationship, remember?"

While Priya and Rahul were bickering, things were not very good in Rajeev and Nikita's love life either, especially after Rajeev switched on the news channel. "Is Nikita the new gold-digger in Bolly town, and who is her new victim? Rahul Saxena answers it all through his new album," the headline blasted as soon as the television was switched on, making Rajeev squirm. He tried to switch off the television, but Nikita had already snatched the remote from his hands, saying, "I want to listen to this."

While Nikita watched the full interview, Rajeev could only look at her with concern and dread in his eyes, at a loss for words to calm her down. However, after the news, Nikita was surprisingly calm and went towards the bed to sleep without saying a word.

Rajeev followed her and held her hands as he asked, "You do know he wants you to react and get some publicity for his new album, right?"

Nikita laid down on the bed without replying and kept staring at the ceiling when her phone beeped with a message notification. "It's Priya. She wants us to come to some get-together they've arranged for her discharge from the hospital. If I don't go, they will think I am hiding from those allegations, and they will win. If I do go, they will again ask all these questions to fuel this controversy. Perfect! Kill me now," Nikita muttered under her breath as she put her hands over her eyes and tried to sleep it off.

THIRTY
RAJEEV GOES BALLISTIC

"Think about it again. We don't have to go if you're not comfortable," Rajeev nudged Nikita, who was standing near the mirror getting ready for the party. She gave him a side glance and replied, "Why should I hide from these people if I haven't done anything wrong? They're putting me down through shady news articles and interviews that their journalist friends are printing. I want to show them that they don't affect me."

Rajeev moved toward the door and said, "It looks like you just want to show Rahul that you are happy with another guy. Anyways, I'm going to bring the car around front, so come quickly." Nikita started to say something, but Rajeev was gone by then.

As soon as they reached Rahul's apartment, Nikita rushed out of the car to avoid the uncomfortable awkward silence of their car ride. Rajeev didn't approve of her reconnecting with the people she had promised to leave behind when they got married. The place was overflowing with the music industry crowd that she hardly knew, so

Nikita tried to find Priya in the chaos.

Rahul was surrounded by people congratulating him on the success of his album, but he kept his eyes glued to the door. He immediately smirked as the person he had been waiting for walked in. He pretended to talk to the crowd surrounding him, waiting for that person to come to him, but minutes passed, and he had to look around, only to find her talking to Priya instead.

"Hey, I cannot apologize enough, and you have no idea how guilty I feel for what happened. It won't be sufficient if I say sorry every day to you, but for what it's worth, I am really happy you have recovered well. I just wanted to see you once, so I came. I will be out of your life for good, and such situations will never happen again because of me. I can promise that," Nikita said earnestly, holding Priya's hands.

Priya dragged Nikita to her bedroom and said, "Just sit here and relax. I'll bring something to eat, then we'll talk." Nikita was pacing up and down the room when she heard Rahul, "It really takes a special kind of impudence to show your face again after what you have done."

Nikita rolled her eyes as she replied, "I just wanted to apologize to Priya properly for once.I have no interest in talking to you, and after today, I'll be out of your lives for good. So just relax."

Rahul was not ready to give up on his taunts, "So, what kind of gifts did it take to buy you off, or did you jump into bed for free? At least you should have been smart enough to ask for private jet flights to Europe or a huge diamond ring," he said, lifting her hand to find no ring on her finger.

Nikita snatched away her hand. "You needn't worry about my marriage gifts. If you have a problem with my being here, then I will leave," she said, almost turning to go, but Rahul caught her. He cupped her face with both of his hands and kissed her.

Nikita pushed him off as she shouted, "What the hell, Rahul?" "Let's go home," she heard Rajeev's voice behind her. Nikita blinked and started stuttering as she tried to explain, "I don't know why he did it. It completely caught me off guard." Rajeev kept staring at her and repeated, in a calm, low voice, "Let's go."

The entire car ride back was suffocatingly silent, with Nikita's attempts to speak being swiftly shut down by Rajeev's raised hand. When they arrived home, Rajeev got out of the car, came to her side, and opened the door. Before Nikita could step out, he firmly grabbed her arm and almost dragged her inside. The dragging continued until they reached their bedroom. Nikita stood quietly as Rajeev paced back and forth, trying to calm himself down. His anger was palpable, and she could feel the tension in the air.

Just as Nikita tried to speak, Rajeev blurted out, "Everything till now has been as per your wish. You wanted to use me to make Rahul jealous. I said ok. You wanted to be friends. I said ok. You were not comfortable staying here, so we had a marriage. We didn't even get close until days after our marriage just because you were not ready. I told you before, if you want to be with Rahul, you have my blessing, but you kept making me a fool and kept clinging on to me. I told you clearly, I am not the person you can mess with, but you decided to make me a backup option just like Rahul made you. I told you to be sure before you come close to me, but you kept taking me for granted."

Nikita tried to gather her strength and said, "He caught me unaware," but before she could complete, Rajeev grasped her throat and pushed her to the wall. "Do you think I am the kind of guy you can play games with and fool around? You need to find someone of your or your darling Rahul's level to play around with, but don't even dare mess with me. I will make sure that it becomes the worst mistake of your life."

The intensity of his hold on her neck kept increasing and ended with a slap and a push. Nikita was too shocked to speak anything as she fell to the ground and stayed there, staring at him. The anger didn't subside there and she was too scared to run.

Rajeev left the room, breaking vases in his path and banging the door shut behind him. Nikita, bruised and terrified, dragged herself to find her phone. With trembling hands, she called Rahul, but her calls went unanswered. Desperation surged through her as she managed to write, "HELP, SAVE ME. HE IS GOING TO KILL ME," before she heard Rajeev returning. She sent the message via text and WhatsApp just as Rajeev lunged forward, snatching the phone away.

In his anger, he threw the phone to the ground and stomped on it repeatedly, ensuring it was unusable. The only relief for Nikita was that this act seemed to have calmed Rajeev down momentarily. Without saying a word, he left the room again, leaving Nikita crouching in the corner in fear.

Minutes felt like hours as Nikita remained in the corner, trembling and afraid Rajeev would come back. Her body ached from the assault, and her mind raced with thoughts of what might come next. Exhaustion and pain eventually overtook her, and she fell asleep on the floor.

In the morning, Nikita was woken up by Rajeev trying to lift her up. She got scared and crouched back in her corner, so he sat near her and said, "It is difficult for me to see my wife kissing another guy, but I thought about it, and I know

Rahul is your first love since school. It's okay if you want to go back to him, as I cannot force you to like me."

Nikita kept staring at Rajeev, who was speaking with his head down, fiddling with his fingers in nervousness. The fiddling stopped, and his head shot up, a beaming smile slowly spreading across his face, when she replied, almost stammering, "I don't love him... and I'm not going to him."

Nikita tried to get up but almost fell again due to weakness in her knees. She pushed away Rajeev's hands, who had rushed to help her. She managed to climb onto the bed and covered her face with pillows, trying to sleep, but was woken up immediately by Rajeev, who was trying to put ointment on her bruised neck and hands. She tried to brush off his hands again, but he refused to give up and kept applying the ointment.

After a few futile attempts to push him away, she closed her eyes and surrendered to the ointment application, feeling quite sore from the previous night's chaos. The room was filled with an awkward silence, broken only by the sound of Rajeev's careful ministrations.

Rahul had thrown his phone in the cupboard at night when he kept receiving calls from Nikita. He knew his plan of causing a fight between her and Rajeev had worked, but if he picked up the call, she might want him to come and resolve things, which he was in no mood to do.

He got up in the morning and tried to check his phone but backed out, as he wanted to avoid Nikita and irritate her more. He remembered how angry she used to get when he forgot to call her back after seeing her missed calls. He smiled and continued to clean up the after-party chaos from last night. He saw Priya smiling after days and decided to devote some time to her, as only a few days had passed since her recovery.

It was nearly night when they both finished making their house livable again and plopped on the bed. Rahul finally decided to check his phone and was a little disappointed to see no new missed calls from Nikita after the night.

He then searched for the message from her and sighed in relief when he found one, but that sigh of relief turned into a frightened gasp as he read it. He kept trying to call her phone, but it was saying switched off while Priya kept asking him about his sudden change of expressions and visible exasperation in his behavior. He showed her the message as he started getting ready in haste, "I have to check on her. Why is she not picking up the phone?" Saying this, he ran out of the house.

Rajeev had spent the entire day taking care of Nikita — not so much out of guilt, but in the hope that she would finally talk to him again, since she hadn't spoken a word all morning. He was pressing her legs and continuously staring at her when he got a call from his security. "Rahul is here. I think he wants to meet you," Rajeev said. As soon as Nikita heard this, she immediately got up and went to the bedroom. Rajeev went to the hall and told his security to send Rahul in. As soon as Rahul saw Rajeev, he pounced on him, and punches were flying until Nikita shouted, "Stop it! What is going on?"

Rahul rushed towards her, asking, "Are you okay?" Rajeev noticed that she had changed into a full-length salwar suit and covered her head and neck with a dupatta, hiding her bruises. This intensified his guilt, so he did not stop Rahul from holding her close and asking if she was all right. "I just saw your message. I kept calling you. I was scared out of my mind. Let's go from here. We will go to the police and make sure this guy pays for hurting you," Rahul said, caressing her face and trying to remove her dupatta as he noticed bruise marks near her chin and neck.

Nikita pushed him away, adjusted the dupatta to cover her face again, and said, "I am fine. Don't worry about the message I sent yesterday. We just had a disagreement, so I wrote those things. Sorry for disturbing you, or not, as it clearly took you 24 hours to see a message, so you don't seem to have been disturbed by it. Anyways, thanks for bothering to come, but you can leave now. The issue is resolved."

"Are you out of your senses, Nikki? He has clearly hit you. This is not the time to show me attitude. Just come with me to the police, and we will talk about our problem later," Rahul said, trying to hold Nikita's hands again, but she brushed him off.

"Rahul, leave. It is my internal matter with my husband. Please don't interfere. I sent you the message by mistake. Forget about it and go from here," Nikita replied and left the room. Rajeev was more in shock than Rahul, seeing Nikita take his side after what he had done to her. He told the security to show Rahul out as he stood there, looking incredulously at Nikita leaving the room. He finally rushed to follow her.

"You could have gone with him. You don't have to stay back for me. He seemed really worried about you," Rajeev said sheepishly, standing by the door of the bedroom. Nikita walked towards the door and nudged him out of the room, closing the door on his surprised face. She looked out through her window, only to see Rahul getting into his car, and then tears started rolling down her face.

Rahul sat in his car until his anger and frustration subsided, then turned to give one last look at the house that had destroyed his mental peace before starting the car with the determination never to see that place again.

THIRTY-ONE
GRANDMA TO THE RESCUE

"So how long do you plan on not talking to me?" Rajeev was following Nikita around in the evening when she returned from the office and even followed her to the kitchen where she was looking for something to eat. Nikita looked at him with irritation, which turned into surprise as she saw an aged woman entering the hall. Rajeev also saw her and rushed to touch her feet and hug her, saying, "You shouldn't have taken such a long flight, Dadi. We were going to come to the USA next month."

Nikita also came near to touch her feet, but Dadi stopped her and hugged her, saying, "No need. Your place is in my heart. This idiot didn't tell me on time, and the visa, tickets, and everything combined delayed my visit. Otherwise, I wanted to see your wedding live. No issues, now show me the photos, videos, everything that you have." Nikita forced a smile and said, "Of course, Dadi. I'll get them right away." She glanced at Rajeev, who looked relieved to have his grandmother there as a life saver.

Rajeev watched as Nikita finally smiled and laughed, spending the whole day with his grandmother, discussing their wedding and her life in the USA. The smile vanished as soon as he entered the room and sat near them. Dadi noticed this and asked, "It hasn't even been a month, and this guy has already fought with you? You can complain about everything to me. Don't worry, I will beat him black and blue until he says sorry to you; I will always take your side only." Rajeev left the room, not wanting to spoil the new bond forming between Nikita and his grandmother.

After several failed attempts to understand the reason for their quarrel, Dadi held Nikita's hands and said, "Don't misunderstand his anger. He makes very few close relationships and becomes very possessive about them. He can go to any extent to protect his loved ones because a lot of his own family has left him alone. I'm sure he told you about his mother and father. It deeply affects any child to witness his mother's depression and suicide, and then see his father leave with the person responsible for her death. He has a lot of pent-up anger, which sometimes comes out on his close ones, but try to bear with his few minutes of aggression because, most of the time, he is the most caring guy you will ever meet."

Nikita stared at Dadi, covering her mouth with both hands in surprise. Dadi realized that Rajeev hadn't told her about his past, so she patted her back and said, "It's not a pleasant story, so he doesn't like to talk about it. Rajeev's father was in love with another woman but married his mother mainly for her money and business. He didn't end his previous relationship, and Rajeev's mother couldn't bear such a humiliating life anymore. Rajeev was too young to understand anything as his mother handed him over to her most trusted person, Philip, before taking her own life to escape her troubles. Rajeev hated his father, who wasn't keen on the added responsibility either. I tried to take care of him for a few years, but Rajeev was sent to boarding schools and colleges as his father settled in the USA, and I had to move there too. All this neglect from his own family has made him bitter and over-possessive about his relationships. I hope you will forgive his mistakes and not misunderstand him."

Dadi lay down to sleep and signaled Nikita to leave as she said, "He hasn't talked about anyone for even a minute, but for the past few months, you have been his only topic whenever he called me. He gets angry because he is scared of losing someone close again. He hasn't had anyone who has stayed with him, so he becomes overprotective. His possessive, caring nature gets misunderstood by others. I just hope you are not one of those people."

Nikita smiled as she started pressing Dadi's legs and said, "You should tell me more about him. It feels like I've told him everything about myself, but he has told me nothing about his life. I keep discovering something new every day." Dadi stopped her and replied smiling, "The best way to know him would be to talk to him. Go now and let me sleep. I don't want to come between a guy and his newly wedded bride."

Nikita found Rajeev fast asleep in the bedroom. Impulsively, she hugged him, waking him up. He hugged her back, a smile on his face, but it disappeared immediately when she said, "I am sorry about your mom, dad, and everything. I hope you consider me close enough one day to share your life instead of me getting to know about it from your grandmother."

Rajeev nudged her away as he got up and said, "I don't need your sympathy, and it was all years ago, so I didn't feel it was a necessary discussion point for marriage. You don't have to start talking to me just because you heard my sob story. I am still me, and whatever I do with you has zero connection to my past."

Nikita refused to leave him and hugged him again. He resisted and pushed her away, saying, "Don't do something you will regret later. I don't need this." But Nikita hugged him even harder until he gave in and hugged her back.

Rahul was pacing up and down while venting to Priya, "You should have seen her, Pri. She is literally his slave, too scared to come out of captivity even after being beaten black and blue. I cannot understand how a well-educated, financially independent person chooses to stay with a physically abusive husband. What could he threaten her with? Why is she so scared to leave him? I have been trying to get in touch with his ex-girlfriends, one of whom I had seen when I used to drop off Nikita at his office. None of them want to come forward and talk about him, but I can sense they have been through similar abuse and are scared of him."

Priya, who had grown bored of his daily rants about Nikita, suddenly sat up and said, "Are you telling me that you have been spending your days investigating Nikki's husband's exes? Have you lost it completely, Rahul? Nikita is highly educated and knows how to file a police case if she needs to. You and I don't need to meddle in her personal life."

Rahul gave her an exasperated look and said, "I had no idea you've started hating your childhood friend so much that even when I told you I saw marks of physical abuse on her neck, you don't even have the slightest sympathy for her."

Priya sighed and replied, "I don't know what you saw, but bruises can be caused by many things. Rajeev is a little rough in bed, so maybe it was that or some other minor accident. If it was physical abuse by Rajeev, I doubt that Nikki would still be staying with him. She is not the one to be intimidated by anyone. I think you have forgotten your own childhood friend's characteristics."

She stopped talking as she saw Rahul gaping at her, then he asked the most awkward question, "How do you know that Rajeev is rough in bed?" Priya stammered as she tried to collect her thoughts and come up with a convincing answer but failed to think of anything.

Rahul held her by her arms and shook her while glaring, "HOW?" For the first time, Priya was scared of Rahul and started stuttering when she replied, "I was angry at Nikki trying to get close to you. I knew she liked Rajeev and so I did what I did. I wanted to hurt her as she was hurting me. I think Rajeev also wanted to make her jealous, so he agreed, but we both felt guilty afterward and decided not to tell anyone. It just happened in the heat of the moment due to our jealousy. It meant nothing, Rahul."

Rahul brushed off Priya as she tried to hug him, which broke her down and led to her uncontrollable weeping. "When was this and how rough?" Rahul asked, unperturbed by her crying. "I don't remember exactly. I think it was when you told her not to hang out with Rajeev so much and got upset about her growing closeness with him. One day, I saw you both hugging, and it really upset me. I know we don't have a very exclusive relationship, but emotionally, I didn't like seeing you affected by anyone other than me. Nikki's behavior started affecting you too, and I think her closeness with you was making Rajeev jealous. We both felt like we were facing similar rejection, and that's what led to the mistake happening," Priya held Rahul's hand, trying to explain herself.

Rahul wasn't in the mood to listen to her explanation. He shrugged off her hands again and shouted, "What did you mean by 'he is rough'?"

Priya shook her head as she replied, "You know how some people are— he's assertive and gets what he wants, even if the other person isn't comfortable. I think they had an argument or a fight and she just called you out of habit. Then she realized it was a personal matter and didn't want to pursue it further, so she backed out when you came to help."

Rahul held his head in frustration. "The point of an open relationship is to be open about what we do. I won't even get into your lying and hiding things, but at least have the decency to talk to a girl who was once your friend and roommate. You know that guy is dangerous, and yet you're okay with her living with him. I've never asked you to be an exclusive, loyal girlfriend, but I do expect basic humanity from you towards a friend. Is that too much to ask?"

Priya reluctantly picked up her phone and dialed Nikita. "Hey Nikki, I wanted to talk. We didn't get a chance to talk properly last time at my party, so I thought we could connect if you're free. I can come by your house this weekend if you're not busy."

Priya hung up and looked at Rahul. "She will call me back. I'll talk to her and try to bring her here. Then we can figure out what to do legally if that guy has been abusive towards her." She reached out to touch Rahul's face to calm him, but he brushed it off and went to the bedroom, slamming the door shut behind him.

THIRTY-TWO
RAJEEV DRAGGED TO THE COURT

Priya was amazed looking at a bubbly Nikita, who was refusing to let go of Rajeev's hands as she conversed with her. "I am so glad you came, and you cannot imagine my happiness seeing that you don't hate me like Rahul. I thought you both would never want to see me again, but here we are. I would have come to meet you there, but I don't want to create a scene with Rahul as his hatred increases a notch each time, he looks at me," Nikita said.

Rajeev could sense the reluctance in Priya's behaviour, which might be due to his presence, so he excused himself to get some snacks. Priya waited for a few minutes to ensure Rajeev was out of earshot and then held Nikita's hands as she whispered, "Nikki, if the guy is hitting you, just say the word, and I will call the police. You can leave right now with me. You don't have to be scared, as I am with you."

Nikita laughed and caressed Priya's hands as she replied, "Rahul told you a wrong story. He saw some marks on my hands which happened during a scuffle. It was just a small heated moment, after which Rajeev didn't stop apologizing until I forgave him. He takes care of me a lot, and sometimes I think he loves me more than I love him, so don't worry about me."

Priya smiled as she left Nikita's house, relieved that Nikita's happiness with Rajeev meant she would stay far away from Rahul for good. Everything was finally working out as per her plan, but she hoped against hope that Rahul would stop meddling with Rajeev's past girlfriends. Nikita was head over heels in love with Rajeev and out of her way now; only Rahul needed a bit of guidance to come back on her path.

As soon as Priya entered her flat, she found an ecstatic Rahul who jumped on seeing her and ran to hold her in an embrace. She couldn't help but smile, thinking maybe she didn't need to worry about Rahul after all. But her happiness was short-lived when Rahul explained the reason for the hug, "I finally managed to convince one of his exes to file a case against him. She is the most recent one, whom he dumped because of Nikki. She was caught quite unaware with the marriage, as she says he was with her just a week before. Anyways, she wants revenge, and I will help her with that."

Priya saw Rahul prancing around in happiness and asked, "Why exactly are you doing this? I met Nikki, and I have never seen a person more in love than she is now. She said they both had a misunderstanding and have cleared it. Don't spoil her life which has just started."

Rahul froze in his tracks and gave Priya a disgruntled look with both his hands on his hips. "You thought she was in love with me just few weeks ago and were so convinced that you tried to kill yourself, but now you want to convince me that you think Nikki is in love with some other guy?"

Priya shrugged her shoulders. "I made a one-time mistake that I would always regret. However, you going after Rajeev is more due to jealousy and less due to your concern for Nikki. Nikki needs no saving. I saw her happy married life today. There is no place for Rahul and Priya in there. She is completely surrounded by Rajeev's love, his world, and even his grandmother's affection. So just let them be, and we both should spend some time together, which we lost in hospital trips."

Rahul rolled his eyes as he replied, "That guy is amazing to have convinced two dumb girls that physical abuse is some kind of love, but I still have a brain, unlike both of you. I need to call that girl and work out her legal plan. You can continue fantasizing about Nikki and Rajeev's fictional, non-existent love story."

Nikita woke up in the morning to Rajeev staring at her and caressing her hair. "You scared me a little. What happened? Why do I feel like you're preparing me for some bad news with this extra pampering?" Nikita smiled and asked as she stopped his hand from caressing her. Rajeev lay down beside her and said, "Do you remember the girl you saw me with in our office when we had that fight in my cabin?" "The one where you shouted at me? Yes, I think I remember that vividly. What about her?" Nikita replied with a smile.

Rajeev moved towards her, hugged her, and hid his face on her shoulders as he spoke, "She has filed a case against me for physical abuse, cheating, and a whole lot of other things. I wanted you to hear it from me before this gets blasted all over the media, which your Rahul is making sure happens. I was meeting her on and off, but it wasn't a serious relationship. I have cameras all around my office and house specifically to avoid this issue, and I also have other written proof that whatever we were doing was consensual. But before I can prove it in court, the media is going to make me look like a criminal. I found out that Rahul is helping her with her case and especially handling the media as PR for her, so even before the court does anything, I will be proven guilty in the media."

Nikita smiled as she held his face with both her hands and then kissed his forehead, saying, "I trust you completely. If you say she is wrong, then I believe you. I cannot believe that you would ever harm anyone. I just don't understand Rahul's motive in all this. I didn't know he hated me so much that, just to hurt me, he would start attacking my husband. I should say sorry to you. If I wasn't here, the media and Rahul would have stayed out of your life."

Rajeev was surprised by her blind trust in him and stopped himself before confessing any more. He liked how she trusted and supported him, so he decided he didn't want to lose that by stating unrelated facts of the past. If it came out during the case, he would deal with it then.

Rajeev was right about one thing: all types of media had started hounding him even before the case went to court. As Nikita switched on the TV, there were hour-long specials with headlines as Nikita's husband was a playboy, showing edited footage of him assaulting women. Social media was no different, with crude morphed pictures of Rajeev with multiple women and a few cartoon characters depicting him as an abuser. She threw her phone in frustration just as Rajeev came out of the washroom. He looked at her and said, "You don't have to go to court with me. It will only get worse."

Nikita got up to hug him and said, "This is happening because of me. I can't even imagine how you're managing to stay so calm about it. When they were bullying me in the media, you were the only one who stood by me, so I need to be there with you, especially since it's happening because of me."

This was just the beginning of weeks of torture; the court was worse than the media. The allegations and counter-allegations went on in court, with each evidence analyzed exhaustively. The media doubled that analysis, with women's rights activists being openly towards Rajeev. He even had to hire protection for himself and Nikita, but each day he was more concerned about how Nikita was handling it. "It is not true. You know that, right? I know it looks bad, but it was not a serious relationship for me or her," Rajeev would say these things every day after court, and Nikita would just smile and repeat, "I trust you more than myself."

The lawyer looked nervous as he sat with Rajeev and Nikita, explaining the case progress, "The public sentiment is turning against you, even if she doesn't have proof. It's hard for a judge to let you go scot-free, so we need to swing public feelings in your favor. A guy with all financial resources fighting a single struggling model doesn't look good. However, a girl can fight another girl, and no one will object. We need to put Nikita on the stand to explain how beautiful her relationship with you is and how it made both your exes jealous. This is the story we need to spin if we have to win without getting burnt in the process."

Rajeev shook his head as he replied, "I don't want to drag her into all of this. She was not even aware of the situation, and now she will lie in court. I don't want to put this on her. Think of another workaround."

Nikita got up and replied, "There is no lie. I am ready to speak the truth. I am perfectly happy with him, and if that girl had issues with whatever imaginary abuse she was facing, then she should have left him and not the other way around. She can't file two opposite cases, first of abuse and then of cheating. You either were in a happy relationship, or you were not, but stop blaming my husband." The lawyer got up with a smile on his face and told Rajeev, "I don't think we even need to coach her. Let's do it then, Nikita."

Rajeev was nervous throughout her testimony, constantly fiddling with his fingers and casting side glances at Rahul. Nikita was unfazed by the attention around her and kept bashing Rahul on the stand, highlighting his jealousy after her marriage, his collaboration with Rajeev's ex, and how he was spinning stories to create this mess both inside and outside the courtroom. Rajeev smiled as she painted him as the most ideal husband on the planet and expressed her gratitude for his support in her personal and professional challenges.

The lawyer congratulated Rajeev, saying, "This case would have ended sooner if we had called ma'am to the stand earlier." Rajeev smiled and thanked him as he embraced Nikita, but his expression changed when he saw Rahul approaching them. Rahul smirked and shook his head, saying, "You both deserve each other. I was trying to save you from his physical abuse, but you are such an idiot that you have closed that door forever. If you ever try to file a case against him again, because I know this guy is going to hit you again, no court is going to believe you. You haven't harmed me. You've just closed the door on your freedom and happiness forever. I always thought you were an emotional fool, but today you proved it by doing this just to spite me."

Nikita tugged at Rajeev's arm and signaled him to move as she replied, "Thanks for your concern for my happiness, the same concern you showed by not picking up my phone that day and then not calling me back for 24 hours. You must have been really concerned that something would happen to me, so you didn't bother to check if I was alive. Anyway, I solved my problem that day on my own, and I will do the same in the future. Even if I don't, you need not worry about it. I decided to delete you from my emergency contacts after that day." Rahul opened his mouth to retort but decided against it and just watched Nikita and Rajeev leave with their hands entwined.

THIRTY-THREE

THE FAKE SUICIDE STORY UNRAVELS

Priya was sleeping with her legs on Rahul's lap as he watched the news. "So, what else have you not told me? Just like you hid Rajeev's love story, are there any more guys that you hooked up with and forgot to mention to me? I'm a little curious, as I thought we were in an open, honest, sharing kind of relationship, so full disclosure should be rule one for such a relationship to work," Rahul asked nonchalantly, his eyes glued to the TV screen.

Priya woke up with a startle, fumbling for a while before managing to reply, "Nothing, no one. I thought we were over that issue. It was a one-time thing, and I saw how much you hate Rajeev, so I didn't tell you about it. It was just an impulsive reaction, which came out of jealousy against Nikki. It didn't mean anything, and there is definitely nothing else that I have hidden from you."

Rahul kept looking at the TV and started changing channels as he replied, "Sure, I trust you. What is there not to trust, right? I have one more query as I am still confused: if you knew about me and Nikki before and were so angry that you slept with Rajeev out of revenge, then how come you displayed the same anger when you saw us for the second time and slit your wrist as a reaction? The same level of anger came out twice? Actually, I feel like giving you a standing ovation that you managed to be angry with the same intensity on seeing the same event twice."

Priya's mouth opened in shock, and it took her a few minutes to come up with a response, "I had started thinking that you didn't like her in that way, as you were being nice to me, so I let it go. I thought I was making baseless assumptions and I should give you the benefit of the doubt, but then I saw you being so close to her again, and all my assumptions came true, leading to my impulsive suicide attempt."

Priya felt a chill run down her spine as she heard Rahul's words. "I don't think 'impulsive' is the correct word when you spent days searching for videos and articles on how to slash your wrist without causing any significant damage. I think the word you want is 'well-researched.'" Rahul smiled at her and continued, "I thought you were smart enough to know how to clean your search history, but maybe you thought I was too lovestruck and dumb to bother with these things. Actually, you're not wrong there—I wouldn't have bothered to check anything if this Rajeev case hadn't happened. We got so many media handles involved in creating Rajeev's negative image, but neither Nikita nor Rajeev approached a single media person to clear their stand. Surprisingly, Nikita, the same person who had leaked your suicide story immediately to get attention, didn't do anything this time. Something just didn't add up."

Priya started to speak, but Rahul signaled her to stop as he continued, "This was the situation where she should have used her media contacts to save themselves before the media trial, but she used her media contacts when you cut your hand. That incident actually hurt her reputation more while people attacked her flat, so I'm still trying to figure out the reason she took such a step which had no visible benefit to her. The only explanation is that she didn't. She knew no one. I've been managing her since school—her photoshoots, music video work, media interviews—everything was handled by me through my team. She never talked to anyone, or rather, I never let her do anything, so there was no way she developed these media and industry contacts suddenly without me being aware of it. However, there was one person who had all the contacts and who did everything without me being involved—my darling Priya." Rahul smiled at Priya with almost a twinkle in his eyes.

Priya tried to hold his arms, but he brushed her off. She ran to hug him and started blabbering, "You're taking it all wrong. I don't know what happened with the flat attack, I was in the hospital. You can't seriously think that I faked it all. You saw me in the ICU, covered with all those drips and pipes, but you still think I was lying to you?"

With that, Priya started weeping. Rahul gave a hysterical laugh and tried to speak between fits of laughter, "That's where you made me a fool, sweetheart. I kept thinking you couldn't have done it because your slit wrist and blood were all real, so I kept blaming Nikita. But then you confessed about Rajeev and your relationship, and the actual drama became a little clearer. I admit it took me some time to piece the events together, but hey, better late than never."

Rahul came close to Priya, cupped her face with his hands, and looked intently into her eyes as he said, "You made me such a big fool. Both the girls in my life were taken away by that lowlife pervert, and I still have no idea how all that happened right under my nose. Rajeev was the last piece of this puzzle. You gave him all the ammunition, and he fired the gun. I feel he was the one who orchestrated the media news leak followed by the attack on the flat so Nikki would be forced to leave and go to his house. The rest was not that difficult to figure out—situations were created, with both of you adding fuel to the fire after the misunderstanding between Nikki and me started. Rajeev doing all this deceitful act is still okay for me as he hardly came into our lives a year ago. But Priya, we have known each other since we were kids. For once, we could have just talked. I used to think we both were in one of the most mature, progressive, trusting relationships that no one else needed to understand but us. I was so wrong!"

Priya replied with a smirk, "How conveniently you've put everything on me when you fell in love with my only friend and roommate. Nikki was the only person who stood by me after school and wasn't jealous of my fame, career, looks, and boyfriend. But you came and spoiled it. I didn't have a problem with Nikki liking you—as so many girls have liked you since school and still fawn over you even now. I had a problem when you fell in love with Nikki, Rahul. You fell in love with Nikki, and I don't know if you were lying to yourself, but you kept lying to me and Nikki just so you could keep both of us around you. So, please, I don't need a morality lecture on our relationship from you as you were the first one to break it. I am not sorry for what I did, as there is no way you can make a person fall out of love if that love keeps trotting around in the flat next door. Rajeev was ready to move that problem away from my sight for good, so I joined hands with him. I don't regret even 1% of what I did."

Rahul sat down with his hands covering his face, "I guess you are right. I am just tired of looking for answers about who did what. I have been running around finding the truth about Rajeev's and your actions, spent days searching the online activity of you both to get clues, but in all of this, I just realized that it all started with me. I gave everything to Nikki, but I was scared to give her the only thing she wanted—commitment. She said yes to the first guy who offered her marriage, but gives her no other happiness, abuses her daily, and has been deceitful throughout. Still, his commitment meant more to her than my love. I don't blame you or Rajeev for anything. Frankly, I don't care, as you both would have been able to do nothing if I wasn't scared of my love. I love her, Pri. I'm sorry, but I love her. I have to, and I will sort out everything. It should have been a discussion between just Nikki and me, but at least now I won't let anyone come between us."

As Rahul tried to leave, Priya held his hand and spoke in a very low but stern tone, "Think before you take any rash step—it will be either her or me."

Rahul turned once before leaving the flat and gave a chuckle as he replied, "I wish I had decided sooner, as she has been the only one for me. You were just a friend, Pri, and you will always be close friend. But Nikki was raw and honest with me. She never hid her feelings and spoke what was on her mind. I wish I had done the same. I can't spend my life decoding your actions and finding ways to keep you pleased at the cost of my happiness. Because even if you are close to me, you will always be just a friend. Anyways, you have a lot of sycophants around you, so you won't miss me much. But I need to have someone I miss, back in my life."

THIRTY-FOUR

THE FATEFUL ASSAULT

"What is wrong with you, Rahul? Will you stop calling me? I don't want to see your proof," Nikita cut the call and looked around to make sure Rajeev had not heard it. Rahul had been badgering her for two days with his baseless accusations about Rajeev. She ignored it at first but now it had started affecting her. She stared at Rajeev's phone on the table, looked at the door, repeated this thrice, and then decided to pick up his phone. The passcode was her birthday, so it wasn't very difficult to break, although it made her doubt Rahul's words again. "Why would Rajeev do all that to hurt me, as Rahul claims, and still keep my birthday as the passcode?" Nothing was making sense, but until she proved Rahul's theories wrong, she knew she wouldn't be able to sleep.

There were a few calls to an unknown number on the day Priya was taken to the hospital and also the day after when people had attacked her house. As she was noting it all down, Rajeev entered the room and looked at her quizzically.

"I was checking for Philip's number as I needed to order something," Nikita replied nervously. Rajeev came near her and started playing with her hair as he took his phone away. Nikita kept staring at him, fidgeting with her fingers, and for a second her breathing stopped as he suddenly looked at her with wide eyes. "Dadi had called, and I missed it. She was traveling and might have needed something. I will just try to find out," he said as he left the room.

Nikita knew he would be busy for some time, so she started going through his laptop search histories. Rahul had been calling her continuously to convince her about his Priya-Rajeev collaboration theory, but she was unable to believe it. She needed proof to disprove Rahul's accusation.

Rajeev entered the room and quietly stood behind Nikita, who was scrolling through his bank account statements. Nikita was startled as she heard Rajeev's voice behind her, "If you wanted to know how rich I was, you just needed to ask once."

It took some time to collect her thoughts, then Nikita replied, making bold accusations, "Why is there a payment to the media house on the 10th? You don't handle direct payments from your personal account to the media for work, so this cannot be official. This is the main media house that first leaked Priya's suicide news, and the rest of the portals copied it. So, why are you giving these people such a huge amount? Don't even bother to lie or change the topic. I want a straightforward answer."

Rajeev's eyes remained steady, without the slightest flicker. He pulled her hand and made her sit on the bed as he spoke calmly, "I wanted to show you the real face of Rahul—how he doesn't care about you and how easily he will choose Priya over you in any situation. I wanted you to find the truth and couldn't think of a better way. I know you got hurt in this whole fiasco, but it was necessary for you to realize how Rahul was treating you as his backup plan."

Nikita brushed off his hands, shaking her head, "Please tell me that you didn't become a puppet of Priya. Wait a minute, wait a minute. Did you plan that stone throwing at my flat too? I didn't know that you wanted me to get hurt that bad." Rajeev scratched his head as he replied, "I was nearby. I wouldn't have let any stone touch you.".

Nikita stared at Rajeev, hands on her hips, "What about you and Priya?" Rajeev sighed deeply, "It was a one-time thing." Before he could finish, Nikita shook her head again and turned to her cupboard, pulling out her clothes. Rajeev tried to reason with her, insisting it meant nothing to him, but Nikita continued packing. "You are overreacting," was the last thing Nikita heard before brushing off Rajeev's hand with disgust and walking out of his house.

Now, sitting in Rahul's car with her hands covering her face, Nikita replied, "Rahul, please stop. I didn't call you to hear about how horrible Rajeev is or how wrong I was. I agree that your story was right. He and Priya orchestrated everything, but it doesn't change how you behaved with me after the drama started by them. You chose her and thought I was wrong. I don't want to prove anything, but Priya colluding with Rajeev and you abusing me for causing Priya's suicide are not very different for me. No one is a saint here."

Rahul glanced at her as he drove, but seeing the frustration on her face, he didn't dare to reply. "I am not going back to this house," Nikita screamed when she saw Rahul stopping the car at his flat. "Just drop me at a hotel nearby."

Rahul cupped her face with his hands and said, "Just give me a chance to talk, and then you can go anywhere you want." As they climbed the stairs, Rahul suddenly turned and said, "Priya is not living with me. Her parents were in town, so she has shifted there."

Nikita cut him short, "I don't care. She doesn't exist for me. She just has to have whatever I like. When I wanted you, she wanted you. Even when you've been in a casual relationship for years, she just couldn't see you liking me. When that guy in school liked me, she made sure he fell in love with her. When I liked Rajeev, she had to go and sleep with him within a day of meeting him. She just can't stand any guy liking me. The Priya chapter is over for me."

Rahul opened his flat and pulled her in, saying, "Just come here for a while and let me explain. First of all, I told you to forget about that suicide incident. Didn't I say we would never talk about it? Second, you shouldn't judge Priya for this; it was kind of my fault. I tried to keep both of you around and really messed it up. I knew I had fallen hard for you, but I didn't want to lose Priya, so I didn't tell her anything. I should have come clean in front of both of you; then this disaster of your marriage would have easily been avoided."

Nikita brushed off his hands and stood still in the hallway, replying timidly, "I told him everything about school, especially that incident."

Rahul stared at her, his neck moving forward automatically in shock as he shouted, "Are you an idiot? You told that guy about the incident involving us? Do you have any idea how he can use that against us? Were you out of your senses? That guy literally got people to throw stones at your house, and you gave him ammunition to destroy you further. I have never seen a bigger fool than you in my life."

Nikita replied hesitatingly, "I didn't want to start a new relationship by hiding my past." Rahul pulled at his hair in frustration, saying, "The past means ex-boyfriends or any diseases, not a crime you committed with other accomplices, endangering all of them by making them susceptible to future jail time."

Nikita made a sad face and tried to hold his hand, but Rahul's anger was uncontrollable. "Do you have any idea how cunning that guy is? And you told him such a big secret. He's a businessman, and he knows exactly how to use a person's vulnerability to his advantage. We are not exactly on the same team here, so I can't even imagine how he will use this information. But one thing is sure: he will use it to destroy us."

After several minutes of resisting, Rahul gave in to Nikita's repeated attempts for a hug. She said meekly, "Maybe he forgot about it. I told him long ago, and he didn't even ask for any further clarifications. We took care of the issue long ago, so I doubt anyone can uncover anything new about the case. It was a one-time mistake, like you thinking Priya's suicide attempt was real."

Rahul looked at her in amusement and replied, "Yes, you won't let me forget that ever. However, I don't have a good feeling about Rajeev. I feel wary of him, and rightly so. Hopefully, you're not thinking of going back to him." Nikita tickled him until he fell on the bed, then replied, "I don't want to talk about him. Can we talk about something else?"

When Nikita woke up, it was already past midnight. She didn't realize that they both had fallen asleep while talking. She thought it would be awkward to stay in the same flat as Rahul and decided to move her stuff back to her old place. She carefully pushed aside Rahul's legs, which were near her, and picked up the keys to her flat.

As soon as she switched on the lights at her place, she found Rajeev sitting on the sofa. She put her hands over her mouth to muffle the scream that almost escaped her, but she quickly composed herself and asked angrily, "Why are you in my flat, and how did you even get in without breaking the lock?"

Rajeev's eyes were burning with rage as he moved slowly towards her, causing Nikita to step back in fear. He spoke slowly, his tone low and menacing, "I've been waiting for you for hours to explain my side of the story. I thought you were mad at me, and even though I hate explaining myself, I felt I owed it to you because I felt I made a mistake and you misunderstood me. But I was wrong about owing you an explanation. You're not mad. You just wanted an excuse to go back to your lover. As soon as Priya was out of his life, you couldn't wait to jump into bed with him. So, how does it feel to get the love of your life back? You've been tenacious, I must say, in your attempts to make him jealous, even going to the extent of marrying me. It was a long wait, but you won in the end. Congrats, sweetheart."

"You're taking it wrong. I was just talking—" Before Nikita could finish her explanation, Rajeev grabbed her roughly by her hair and slammed her against the wall, roaring, "Stop playing these games with me. I gave you too much respect by marrying you. You deserve to be treated as Rahul treats you. You can be nothing more than a showpiece. You made the biggest mistake of your life by making me a fool and using me to get to Rahul." He pushed her against the wall again and kept hitting her as he screamed, "You made me a joke in front of the whole world just to make Rahul jealous so that he comes back to you." The anger, the punches, and the shouting didn't stop until Nikita's bloodied body collapsed on the floor. He gave one last kick to her stomach before leaving the flat.

A groggy Rahul collided with Rajeev as he emerged from Nikita's flat. Before Rahul could fully wake up and comprehend the situation, he noticed Rajeev's hand dripping with blood. Shocked into action, Rahul attempted to grab Rajeev, but he pushed him away and walked off.

Rahul hesitated briefly but ultimately decided to check inside the flat; Nikita was already missing from his own flat when he had awakened. His hand instinctively covered his mouth in horror as he felt sick to his stomach upon seeing Nikita's disfigured face, barely visible amidst the blood. Hastily, he pulled a bedsheet to cover her, then immediately called for an ambulance.

Fearful of waiting, Rahul resolved to drive her to the hospital himself, struggling to hold back tears as he sat beside Nikita in the car, dialing the police as he started the engine. "I will kill you, Rajeev. I am going to kill you for this," Rahul muttered to himself, battling to control his anger, his gaze repeatedly shifting to the passenger seat where Nikita lay unconscious.

THIRTY-FIVE

FIR VS THE BLACKMAIL

"Why aren't you listening to me? I saw that guy leaving the house. He's the one who did this to Nikki. Just file the FIR, I'm the eye-witness." Rahul was screaming at the police inspector outside the hospital.

"Sir, with due respect, you didn't actually see the act, and you have a history of filing a false case against Mr. Rajeev. We cannot arrest an influential person without taking madam's statement. The doctor is hopeful that she will wake up in a few hours. Rajeev is a known personality and won't disappear, so please relax and let us take the statement."

Rahul shook his head in frustration and went inside the hospital, only to be intercepted by the doctor. "She's awake and asking for you." Before Rahul could enter the room, the police stopped him. "Let us do our work first for a faster resolution of your FIR."

Rahul was left biting his teeth in anger for over half an hour. When the policeman finally rushed out and left even quicker, Rahul's skepticism grew. Without hesitation, he hurried inside.

Nikita lay awake, her eyes fixed on the ceiling as Rahul entered. "You scared me to death," he whispered. "I've never felt so relieved to see your eyes open. And I've never noticed how beautiful they are—like ocean waves." Rahul smiled softly and leaned in to gently stroke her cheeks.

Nikita replied without looking at him, "He tried to kill me, Rahul. He hates me so much that he wanted me to die. I did so much for him. I fought with everyone for him, and he tried to kill me. I could see it in his eyes when he was hitting me."

"You have a problem that he wanted to kill you? You don't have a problem that he actually tried to kill you? Nikki, are you still not over him?" Rahul looked at her in disbelief.

"I want to see him in jail and make sure he never comes out. I'll put all the money I have, but please get me the best lawyer you know. I want him to feel the same pain he made me feel that night, but it should be delivered by the police," Nikita said, closing her eyes and signaling Rahul to leave.

It took nearly a week for Nikita to get out of the hospital, and the first thing she wanted to do was start her divorce procedure. Rajeev was surrounded by media as he approached the family court, bombarded with questions.

"You're unnecessarily making me famous just because the media's favorite, Rahul, likes to keep filing new cases against me. I'm still trying to make sense of how he manages to convince girls around me to file cases against me. As soon as I figure that out, I can answer all your questions. Till then, let's all discover what Rahul ji has in store for us," Rajeev breezily answered the reporters and went inside the court.

The court proceedings included attempts at counseling them, with suggestions to resolve their issues outside of court. However, Rajeev and Nikita sat silently, glaring at each other with barely concealed anger, refusing to speak a word. Their lawyers eventually urged them to meet outside to negotiate, warning that without a resolution, the case could drag on indefinitely.

Nikita stared at Rajeev with eyes full of hatred as she responded to her lawyer's queries, "There's no need for counseling or reconciliation talks. I don't want to wait for six months. You need to fast-track this case as I cannot keep meeting the guy who tried to kill me."

As Rahul moved closer to wrap his arms around Nikita and console her, Rajeev's anger doubled. He replied through gritted teeth, "You both deserve a standing ovation for first committing adultery and then trying to send the poor victim husband to jail. Unfortunately for both of you, I'm not that dumb. The police you sent, have been hounding me with useless questions about that night you claim I hit you. I actually wanted to discuss the case with both of you."

Rajeev leaned closer as he talked in a threatening tone, "It will be better if you withdraw your complaint; otherwise, Nikita, sweetheart, you will have a lot of your past cases dragged out. For starters, remember the school suicide? You want me to keep my mouth shut, then make sure your police stays away from me. Rahul, I hope you will drill some sense into my darling, Nikita, as she only seems to listen to you now."

Rahul and Nikita looked at each other in shock but waited until the lawyers had left and they were alone in the car. As Rahul started driving, he suddenly banged his hand hard on the steering wheel, shouting, "I knew it. I just knew that rascal would use that story one day, and we gave him the perfect opportunity to blackmail us. Just fantastic!"

Nikita kept hitting her head against the car seat, saying, "I'll ask them to cancel the FIR. It's no use. I don't even want to know what all he has discovered about that school case or how he will use it against us. It's just not worth fighting if we'll lose our reputation over it."

Rahul shook his head in frustration and replied, "One more case we withdraw, one more case he wins. He tried to kill you, Nikki, and I'm unable to do anything. I think you should go ahead with your case and give your best fight, but it's your call. I'll talk to my lawyer about that school case and try to find an escape route so don't worry about us and proceed with your case." Nikita rested her head on his shoulder and said, "It's over." Rahul kept shaking his head in frustration.

Almost a week passed when a dejected Nikita and Rahul barely dragged themselves to the counseling session. As soon as Nikita opened the door, they could hear Rajeev shouting inside. "Why are we wasting time in these out-of-court meetings when we had a perfectly good court session just days ago? I have nothing to discuss. I'm not scared of the court—unlike some people who have committed adultery," Rajeev spat, pacing angrily up and down the meeting room in his lawyer's office.

Before his lawyer could reply, Nikita answered, "After your blackmail attempt at the court, I wanted this meeting with the lawyers. I also have a lot of secrets I could reveal about you, but I am not you who plays dirty in public. I want this to end for good, so let's put all our cards on the table and sign contracts on what can and cannot be revealed. We will then sign these divorce papers and be done with any future interactions. I will withdraw all criminal cases against you, and you sign these non-disclosure agreements that my lawyer has prepared."

As Rahul came close to Nikita and held her waist while he looked over the papers, Rajeev lost his cool at seeing their closeness. He angrily replied, "If you think I am going to pay even a cent to a person sleeping with everyone around, you are highly mistaken. I have all the proof of your so-called loyalty. We are going to court, and I will make you regret the day you met me. You can forget about alimony."

Nikita shook her head in disbelief, "Have you lost your senses? I already regret the day I met you and want to erase every bit of the last year's memory from my life. Why would I take any money from you? I can't believe all this drama was for alimony. You could have just asked me. When did I say I want anything from you? I would even return the gifts you gave me, so just sign these papers and forget we ever met."

Rajeev was taken aback for a while and could not respond, so his lawyer had to take over, "We will look into these conditions and non-disclosures, then contact you accordingly."

Rahul replied on Nikita's behalf, "Fine. You can let us know through our lawyer," and signaled Nikita to leave. As the lawyers exited, Nikita rose and began gathering her bag. Only then did Rajeev finally speak.

"I'll make sure you get your alimony, so you don't have to live off Rahul's money," he snapped.

Nikita fumed when she heard these words and turned towards him, shouting, "You don't have to worry about my finances, but rest assured I will be living with Rahul, and this time it will be in his own flat. You are most welcome to come and punch me to death again. I am not scared of you." She then went to Rahul, who was waiting for her at the door, and impulsively hugged him. She turned back only to smirk at Rajeev.

THIRTY-SIX

THE BATTLE OF THE EXES

"Hey, did you see our paparazzi photos are all over social media?" Nikita came running into the bedroom and plopped down beside Rahul on the bed. She was full of smiles as she flicked through the photos and said, "We actually look good together. Your Pri once told me about this guy who makes sure photos get spread all over the internet and even featured by top media outlets. This will definitely catch Rajeev's attention now."

Rahul's smile, sparked by Nikita's joy, faded the moment he heard Rajeev's name. He gently pushed Nikita away as he tried to sit up, even brushing off her hands when she reached out to stop him. "When will all this end? We've been posing for these paparazzi for weeks just so your husband can see our photos. I want a normal couple's life. If I wanted this media drama, I would have stayed with Pri. Nikki, you really need to decide your priorities—you're slowly turning into Pri."

Nikita settled comfortably among the multiple pillows that decorated Rahul's bed as she replied, "This will go on until he agrees to sign the divorce and non-disclosure papers. He blackmailed me into dropping all charges. I can't let him win at everything."

Rahul shook his head in frustration. "Nikki, you really need to get over him. Since the day we met him for settlement, all I've heard are plans on how to trouble Rajeev. Your whole life seems to revolve around making him jealous, and sometimes I feel like I'm just a prop to you. Any other guy could replace me, and you wouldn't even notice the difference."

Nikita smiled softly and moved closer to him, gently holding his face in her hands. "Are you mad? You are my closest friend. You saved me that day when Rajeev nearly killed me. Of course you're the most important person to me, but this is something I need to do. I can't let Rajeev escape so easily after ruining my life. I hope you understand that."

Rahul raised his eyebrows, a flicker of disbelief in his voice, "Friends? I thought we fought because you wanted more than that. You hated being second to Pri and wanted a relationship beyond friendship. Now we're back to being just friends?"

Nikita shrugged and got out of bed, heading towards the kitchen. She shouted from there while making coffee, "Isn't this what you wanted? You wanted it casual, away from any suffocating commitments. I finally understand you. Marriage is dumb, so let's do it your way. Just fun, no commitments, and no labels for this relationship."

Rahul joined her in the kitchen, and Nikita handed him his coffee as she continued, "Less drama, more fun. I tried my way with Rajeev, and it didn't work. Let's try your way. You and Pri lasted for years. Your approach clearly works better than mine. We can be as open as you want, and you can have your own fun, just like you had all that freedom with Pri. I don't mind."

Rahul smiled, but it didn't reach his eyes, which seemed tired from listening to Nikita's gleeful speech. "You've changed, Nikki, and I don't like it." Before Nikita could reply, her notification beeped. Seeing her smile, Rahul asked, "Is it Rajeev's message?" Nikita looked at him with a beaming face and replied, "Yup. He's right where I want him. Listen to this - 'If you think I'll sign the papers because of your fake paparazzi drama, then you never knew me.'"

Rahul sighed in frustration. "So, where does that leave us? He's not signing, the photos are fake, and I'm dating someone else's wife. This isn't working, Nikki."

"Rahul, will you relax? My marriage is my problem. Out of the two of us, I am the one in an illicit relationship, so don't worry about your moral ethics or whatever image you want to project in front of the media. Everyone will blame me. You, on the other hand, have perfect freedom to continue your life just as it was with Pri, so spare me the lecture and let me deal with my husband my way."

Rahul sat down in the living room with his coffee and replied in an exasperated voice, "How can I relax when I still don't understand what has happened in my life? Some random guy came, and within a few months, he has made my Nikki obsessed with him. I don't even recognize you anymore, even after knowing you for years. Whatever happened in these few months, I may never know, but I don't think my life will ever continue the way it was."

Nikita came and sat down beside him, holding his face with both her hands. She said, "I am trying to be someone you're not ashamed to date, unlike before. I don't want to be the same jealous, clingy person that you were too scared to be with, choosing to continue with Pri rather than date me. I have changed because you never thought the old Nikki was good enough to date in public; I was nothing more than a backup plan."

Rahul held his head with one hand and closed his eyes before replying, "I don't know how many days it will take to cleanse your mind from the garbage that Rajeev fed you about us. You completely forgot our relationship over years and believed some random guy about my feelings for you. How could an unknown person dictate what's happening between us?"

The phone beeped again, and Nikita looked at him with a serious expression. "They've scheduled the domestic violence talk I mentioned for this evening, so I need to leave now. When I come back, we can discuss how there's no external brainwashing, just internal realization, which hopefully you'll also come to understand. For now, I need to focus on exposing my darling husband and his violent behaviour in front of the media. He might try to make me withdraw the case, but he won't stop me from making him a hateful spectacle in front of the entire world. There are more talks lined up about domestic violence awareness, and I'm sure they'll ensure my story gets out there. He's obsessed with his corporate world, so let's see who will want to work with him after I'm through with these talks. How's my plan?"

Rahul shook his head as he saw her enthusiastic, beaming face and replied, "I wish I could bring the same smile to your face as the thought of revenge against Rajeev does. I don't see how these talks will help us when we can't even file a case against him. Despite everyone knowing what he did, he'll never go to jail. It reflects poorly on you that you withdrew the criminal case against him. If we're not pursuing a legal case, all these media trials are pointless; people will forget them in a week. I forgave Pri long ago. For your own sake and peace of mind, I suggest you do the same."

"What a shock that you forgave Pri! What was the alternative? Would you physically hit her or verbally abuse her? Rahul, please, we all know—even Pri knows— that you could never stay angry with her, not even when she cheated on you. You love her too much to keep her out of your life, so 'forgive and forget' is your mantra for her. My mantra is 'never forgive, never forget.' So, whether it's Pri, Rajeev, or any other fights I have, they're my battles alone. I don't expect you to be involved in them. I told you that you have the freedom to live your life your way, and I meant it. One thing: make sure the suicide case from school has no loopholes left to be exploited. I've spoken to the lawyers, and he's sending over the non-disclosures Rajeev had sent. That's your only responsibility—to ensure this case disappears for good. The rest, leave it to me."

As Nikita was leaving the flat for her meeting, Rahul held her hand tightly and said, "Hopefully, after all this, I'll get my old Nikki back—the one who was in love with me, not obsessed with Rajeev." Nikita smiled as she slowly pulled herself away from his grip, saying, "I wish I could get a new Rahul who's obsessed with me and completely oblivious to Pri's existence."

Rajeev flipped through the TV channels which were showing photos of Nikita and Rahul, muttering, "Do any channels show news anymore? They've all become gossip mongers. One paparazzi photo and hours of news segments dedicated to this stupidity." He picked up his phone and dialed Nikita. "If you think this tomfoolery will help you get a divorce so you can marry your Rahul, then you're even a bigger fool than I ever thought you could be."

Nikita smiled as she replied, "It's sad that pictures aren't helping. Alright, I have a better idea. Let's switch to video. Tune in to ABC News at 6 PM, and we'll see if videos work better than pictures. Love you, my dear soon-to-be-ex-husband."

It was nearly dark when Nikita emerged from the news studio and found Rajeev standing outside, leaning against his car. Nikita was taken aback but hid her surprise behind a big smile as she approached him, saying, "I didn't realize I gave such a great interview that the star of my show would come running to congratulate me in person."

Rajeev crossed his arms and smiled as he replied, "Star? I thought you were trying to paint me as more of a villain—wife-beater, domestic abuser, woman harasser. These were a few of the terms used to describe me, without any proof. I'm still contemplating how many zeroes to add to the right of the '1' when I seek compensation after suing you and this embarrassing news channel. Let's discuss it in my car. Let me drop you."

Nikita burst into laughter, which amused Rajeev as he stood there smiling. She replied, "I'm sorry. It's just too funny that you expect me to get into a car alone with you after you tried to murder me not too long ago. Anyway, no thank you, I can manage. You should focus on your PR team instead—how you'll explain these allegations from your wife on national television, along with her cozy photos with someone who isn't you. Your company does not have any progressive people in boardroom, so start saving your job rather than worrying about dropping me home."

Rajeev smirked and said, "Home? How long will that guy's flat be your home? What are you, his 101st girlfriend? You might face housing challenges when Miss 102 comes along. I don't understand why you're putting in so much effort to get a divorce. You were and always will be his backup, and you're soon to be dumped as well, so save your breath."

Nikita got into the cab and turned to reply, "You'll keep getting updates on whether a new Miss 102 has arrived or not through regular paparazzi pictures. So instead of worrying about my relationship status, you should focus on your soon-to-be-dead career."

THIRTY-SEVEN

RAHUL REALIZES THE TRUTH TOO LATE

"When is your dumb plan going to work? Rajeev doesn't seem to be signing any papers soon, and this paparazzi drama needs to stop immediately. I want to have a normal life, a normal relationship, a normal engagement, and finally a normal wedding. We've had enough drama for a lifetime," Rahul said as he watched Nikita getting dressed for another event.

Nikita turned towards him, surprised. "Pump the brakes. What wedding? What engagement? I am not getting married ever again. We have just started dating, Rahul, and we're not even serious about it. I've told you to continue with your life just like you did with Pri because I don't want you to sacrifice anything for our casual dating. My issues with Rajeev are completely separate. It's not like he's going to hand me the divorce papers and we'll rush to the marriage registrar the next minute. Where do you get these ideas?"

Rahul got up and pulled Nikita by her elbow in anger. "What casual dating? You married a guy after knowing him for a few months. We've known each other and lived together for years. Are you seriously comparing our relationship to your infatuation and joke of a marriage that lasted a few days? You just married that idiot to make me jealous. There you go, I admit it. I was jealous, and I realized my mistake. I should never have let you go. We're starting over, and you're still discussing the past. Let's close this Rajeev and Priya chapter and start our own."

Rahul tried to calm himself and reached out to gently caress her hair but Nikita pushed his hand away, looking at him with a mix of surprise and disbelief in her eyes. "Do you have amnesia? You didn't want to be with me—not because you were in love with Priya or anyone else, but because of my so-called 'downtrodden' class. You didn't think I was of your standard, your class, your strata, or whatever. Pri fit perfectly with your image and your family's image. You loved neither of us, Rahul, so stop making a fool out of me like you tried to make a fool out of Pri. Rajeev and my relationship have nothing to do with you either, so stop giving yourself so much importance. We are dating now and getting to know each other. I have forgotten the past, and you should too. Let's start anew."

Rahul threw up his hands in the air and replied in exasperation, "What does it even mean that you have forgotten the past? We have been together for years through all our ups and downs, and you have forgotten that? Yes, I took some time to understand my love for you, and you punished me by marrying that idiot. It still does not change the feelings we had for each other through the years. I have been there for anything and everything you wanted. You can't keep crucifying me for taking time to understand that the feeling I had for you was love."

Nikita came near to stroke his face and hugged him as she replied, "I am thankful that you have helped me throughout these years as a friend, and I have tried to return the favor. We are great friends, and whenever you need me, I will be there for you without even asking, as a friend. However, I don't believe that you loved me all these years, so this dating now is a totally new start for us. Let's not link all these things. Instead, we should just enjoy this time."

As Nikita opened the door to leave, Rahul closed it again and stood leaning against it. Nikita scolded in an annoyed tone, "Will you stop this childish behavior? I have to leave for a seminar. I don't get what your problem is, but this daily whining is getting annoying. We are dating exclusively. I'm not seeing anyone else, so I don't know what else you expect of me. You used to have a problem that I was jealous and clingy. Now I am trying to change that so you can be happy, but you seem to be annoyed by that too."

Rahul rubbed his forehead in frustration as he replied, "Your jealousy showed your love, that you care about me, but this new aloofness makes it look like I am some random guy that you are using as a rebound to get over Rajeev."

Nikita finally pulled at the door, pushing Rahul aside as she moved out. "Rahul, make up your mind. First you want me to be less clingy, then you want me to show jealousy. First you think I am using Rajeev to make you jealous, then you think I am using you to get over Rajeev. You really need to think about what you want instead of telling me what I should do. For now, I really need to go to this seminar." Rahul came out of the flat just to watch Nikita leave. He picked up his phone to make a call. "Pri, can we talk?"

Priya couldn't hide her smile as she sat in Rahul's apartment and said, "I never thought you would forgive me. It feels weird to be back here even though I spent years on this sofa, in this room, and in this flat."

Rahul moved closer, cupped her face with his hands and replied, "I wanted to apologize to you for a long time but finally found the courage today. Seeing the surprise on your face, I know you weren't expecting it, but now I realize this mess was all my fault. I refused to acknowledge my feelings for Nikki, and I kept stringing you along too. I understand how you must have felt seeing me fall in love with Nikki, a feeling of complete helplessness. I feel the same way when I see Nikki in love with Rajeev and can't do anything about it. Your suicide attempt was an extreme step to get my attention, and I blame myself for that. I spoiled all our lives because I refused to acknowledge my feelings. I am sorry it took me so long to understand your situation, because now I am in a similar one. I am in love with someone who is in love with someone else and refuses to acknowledge it."

Priya sat down beside him, letting him rest his head on her shoulder as she patted him. "I know. It is the worst feeling in the world to see the person you love falling in love with someone else and feeling completely powerless to stop it. I would tell you to move on, but it would be hypocritical of me because I am still in love with you."

They were startled by the sound of clapping and saw Nikita standing at the door. "Amazing! I can't even fathom the heights of hypocrisy you've reached, Rahul. After trying to prove not so long ago that I was obsessed with Rajeev, here you are discussing your never-ending love life with Priya. And I don't even have words for Priya. She used to think she was way above me in beauty, class and whatnot, yet she only wants the guys I like. Is there something wrong with your brain that you are so obsessed with me and any guy I date?" Nikita spoke with a smirk on her face.

Rahul stood up and tried to hold Nikita's hands as he spoke, "Will you stop overreacting? Pri is our childhood friend and is just here to listen to me rant. I can't cut her off from my life. She's not some random guy I met a few months ago and got married with."

Nikita brushed off his hands and replied, "Of course not. You both are the role models of healthy relationships. You've stuck together regardless of who else you're dating. That would have been fine if you didn't have the audacity to talk about Rajeev and me, but you just can't stop being a hypocrite. You both make me sick."

Rahul tried to catch her hand to stop her from leaving, but Nikita rushed off. He sighed and threw up his arms in frustration, looking at Priya in desperation. "I just don't know what to do with her. I don't know what to do with myself. And I don't know when I fell so hopelessly in love with her." Priya simply stared at him in silence, her eyes brimming with tears.

THIRTY-EIGHT

A Breakdown & A Confession

As Nikita left the flat, she received a message from Rajeev asking her to meet him at his house because he wanted to talk before signing the divorce papers. She made a face and looked back at the closed door of her flat. Closing her eyes, she could only imagine Rahul and Priya hugging each other to patch things up. Shaking her head in frustration, she looked at her phone message again and became even more determined to visit Rajeev. She was surprised to see that Rajeev was actually standing outside his house when she arrived in the cab.

"I've told Rahul that if I don't come back in an hour, he should call the police, so don't even think of trying to hit me again just because we're alone," Nikita said, making even the cab driver stare back at them in shock.

Rajeev glanced at the driver and pulled her by the arm. "Will you please relax? I just need to talk. Let's go inside.

You've done enough drama in public. I'm sure there are paparazzi around too, so don't worry—no one is touching you."

Nikita rolled her eyes, pulling her arm away from his grip, and walked towards the house. As Rajeev offered her coffee, Nikita tilted her head and looked at him in surprise. "There's no one here to see your pretend care. Just blurt out what you wanted to discuss instead of this civility drama. I know you'd rather bash my head than give me coffee, so just say what you need to say, sign the papers, and we can both go back to living our lives."

Rajeev took some papers out from a drawer and handed them to her. "I've already signed the papers. I've also signed some deposits in your name. You can use them so you don't have to live in someone else's house. I don't care if you're dating that guy, but you need to have your own place and stop depending on men. I also want to talk about some things before we part."

Before he could finish his sentence, Nikita stood up in anger and screamed, "Are you serious? I shouldn't depend on any guy, yet I should depend on your money? Just so you can tell everyone how magnanimous you were to give me alimony? You don't want me to live in Rahul's house but I should shift in a house that you bought? You are unbelievable! I just want to forget you ever came into my life."

Rajeev held her with both hands, almost crushing her in anger. "Will you stop being over dramatic? I can scream louder than you. I don't understand when you started hating me so much that you refuse to see my care for you. I just don't want to see my wife staying with some random guy in his house. If she can't afford a house, then I am willing to buy it for her so that she at least cares about her self-respect, which she has clearly forgotten in her love for Rahul."

Nikita shook her head in frustration. "You don't know when I started hating you? How about the time you punched me and kept hitting me until I passed out and had to spend days in the hospital just to recover from your attack? I would rather live with a guy who has never tried to kill me than take money from a moron who tried to murder me. Leave me. You are hurting me."

Rajeev refused to let her go and shook her in anger, his hands still clasped around her. "If you loved him so much, why did you even bother to come into my life? I told you to think carefully before committing to something so that you don't regret it later. I tried to stay away from you the day you walked into my life, but you kept coming to me. I told you not to say things you didn't mean, but you kept professing your love for me. If you had to go back to Rahul, why did you even come to me in the first place? I warned you not to play games with me, and yet you did it anyway. The very first day I asked you if Rahul was your boyfriend. I did not want to walk this path, but you made me do it anyway, lying all along."

Nikita pushed him away with all her might and gave him a confused look. "What? You didn't even like me back then. When did you try to stay away from me? I told you everything about me from day one, and the Rahul chapter started with your help. You made me realize that I liked him and you were helping me make him jealous. When did I lie to you?"

Rajeev slumped down on the sofa, giving her an exasperated look. "You told me everything? I found out everything about you the day you made me fall in love with you. I found out about you and Rahul. I understood your inclination towards Rahul. You told me nothing until I started asking questions. You kept hiding things from me, and yet like an idiot, I kept falling in love with you. You're right. I wish we had never met. I have never felt so helpless. It is like having an addiction and not being able to overcome it."

Nikita threw her hands in the air in frustration. "How did you find out about things? Were you stalking me? When did you start researching me? Why couldn't you just ask?" Rajeev dug his face further into his hands, mumbling, "As if you would have told the truth."

Nikita sat down and pulled at Rajeev's face to make him look at her. "Neither did you. I am so confused. You need to tell me everything from the beginning. What are you talking about? How did you find out things about me? So, we both started liking each other when we met at the office, but you didn't say anything because your research told you I liked Rahul? And you kept pretending not to like me, even when I kept saying I loved you, because you thought I was lying? Am I getting this right?"

Rajeev shook his head. "Like? I was deeply, madly, idiotically in love, like a fool, and I still am." He hugged her suddenly, his eyes swelling up with tears. Nikita patted his back to calm him. After a while, Nikita gently pushed him back and made him look at her as she said, "I don't know how long I have waited to hear that." Rajeev smiled and pulled her into a tight embrace. Nikita, however, couldn't bring herself to lift her arms to hug him back. She stared ahead with blank, tired eyes, utterly drained by everything.

THIRTY-NINE
BETRAYAL HURTS

As Nikita opened her eyes and turned on the bed, she found Rajeev sleeping beside her. The events of last night rushed back, and she got up in shock. Checking her phone, she saw multiple missed calls from Rahul and realized she had accidentally put her phone on silent. She got up hurriedly, trying to make as little noise as possible, but in the dim light, she knocked over a table clock. The sound woke Rajeev, who rubbed his eyes and saw Nikita staring at him guiltily.

"Where are you going? It's barely 6 a.m. I've never seen you get up so early," Rajeev said, glancing at his watch. "What will I tell Rahul? He'll kill me. I can't face him. I made such a fuss about him and Priya, and now I feel I have cheated on him," Nikita buried her face in her hands, speaking with frustration.

"Hey, I won't let that guy touch even a hair on your head. You don't have to be scared of him. Anyways, what cheating? We are still legally married, so just tell him the truth. Take my phone," Rajeev said, handing her the phone.

Nikita pushed the phone away and moved towards the door, "Are you insane? What am I going to say on the phone? I can't tell him these things over the phone. Don't worry, I'll talk to him. Just stay out of this." Rajeev threw his phone on the bed in frustration and watched helplessly as Nikita left.

As soon as she entered her flat, Rahul ran from the kitchen and hugged her tightly. "Where were you? I was worried sick all night. We have two flats, so if you're angry at me, please go and sulk in the other one instead of disappearing for the night. I made your favorite pancakes because I was sure you couldn't stay mad at me for a long time. Come on in and try."

Nikita looked at Rahul guiltily, avoiding his gaze and glancing around the room. Rahul noticed and said, "If you're looking for Pri, she's not here. I tried to explain to you then, but you stormed off. She just came to talk as a friend and then left. I called her because I felt she was the only person I could talk to after a fight with you. Now I realize that it was a terrible idea because I completely forgot how possessive you can be."

Rahul laughed as he continued, "I almost thought you would scratch both my and Pri's faces, but thankfully, you only slammed the door. It was my last mistake. I won't be discussing us with her in the future. I need to find new friends now!"

He brought a plate full of pancakes and kissed her on the cheek, saying, "Here, my princess. The special blueberry one for you. Please forgive me now. You've punished me enough. I couldn't sleep all night because I was worried sick about you. No more running away, okay?"

Nikita set the plate on the dining table and began fidgeting with her fingers, stuttering as she tried to find the words. "I need to tell you something."

As Rahul hugged her from behind, Nikita fumbled again. Rahul said, "You don't have to say anything. Pri shouldn't have been here. We've only just started dating, and I brought someone into the middle of all that. If there's any issue, we'll solve it, just the two of us. Calling Pri was my mistake, so forget about it."

When Nikita gathered the courage to say, "I need to tell you something urgent about yesterday," Rahul moved toward the bedroom and replied, "Can you tell me while I dress? I need to leave for a recording today. The whole team has finally gathered, so I need to be there on time. Keep talking while I'm dressing so I don't lose time."

Nikita hesitated for a moment and then said, "It's okay. It's not that important. You complete your recording, and we'll talk tonight." Rahul was ready to leave but came near her, held her face with both hands, and said, "Please don't be angry about Pri. We'll sort it out tonight. You know I love you."

As Rahul kissed her forehead and left the flat, Nikita shouted, "I'm not mad about her. She doesn't matter. We'll talk tonight." Their eyes met, and Rahul entered the lift, smiling, while Nikita's smile immediately disappeared as her phone started ringing with Rajeev's name flashing on the screen.

Nikita picked up the call, but before she could reply, Rajeev started screaming, "Where are you? It has been an hour and I was waiting for you to call me. Did you tell Rahul that you don't like him and are leaving him to move back in with me? I think you should shift today since I don't want you to spend another night with that guy."

Nikita replied to his pestering in an annoyed tone, "Can you stop telling me what to do and what not to do? I told you I would handle it, and I will keep my word. You don't have to worry, especially about where I am spending the night."

Rajeev went quiet for a while, then said, "Or maybe you don't want to tell him the truth and keep making a fool out of both of us. Nikita, I am warning you. I can also talk to him if you don't make this right." Nikita cut the call in anger before Rajeev could complete his threat. This made Rajeev lose his mind, and he threw his phone on the bed in frustration.

After pacing up and down in his room for an hour, Rajeev stopped suddenly and picked up his laptop. He glanced through the CCTV camera footage of his house and started checking yesterday's videos. He smiled to himself as he began editing the parts of Nikita's presence in his house, highlighting the timelines. It took nearly an hour, but he was happy with the video. He picked up his phone to forward it to Rahul's number, adding a message before sending the video: "I am not sure how you'll feel about your so-called girlfriend spending the night with me, but hopefully, it should translate into you getting out of her life as soon as possible."

Nikita had decided to cook Rahul's favorite dishes as a gesture of appreciation for his morning pancake surprise, hoping it might also make it easier to talk about Rajeev with him. Her plans came to a halt when Rahul banged open the door, standing there with eyes full of rage. Nikita was surprised to see him and glanced at her watch, "I thought you'd come by evening. What happened? Any issue with recording? Did something happen at work?"

Rahul clenched his fists and closed his eyes, "I just need to know what you were doing yesterday. Where were you? Just one line answer. No explanation, no roundabout stories, just straightforward truth."

Nikita, realizing Rahul knew something, decided to come clean, "I was with Rajeev." Before she could continue, Rahul thrust his phone towards her face, showing a video. Her eyes widened in shock as she saw herself entering Rajeev's house. The video showed her movements in the house with timestamps, clearly from Rajeev's multiple home CCTV cameras.

She had no reply as Rahul screamed in anger, "What were you doing there? Is Rajeev telling the truth? Why didn't you say something this morning while I was frolicking around you like an idiot, apologizing for Pri? All the while you must have been congratulating yourself on how easily you made a fool out of me. What did you think, that you could just keep quiet and I'd never know, all the while making me feel guilty about Pri?"

Nikita tried to calm him down by reaching out to hold him, but Rahul pushed her away, "I just need to hear from you once. Why?" Nikita could only manage to utter, "I am sorry," in a choked voice.

Rahul scratched his head and said dejectedly, "Just get out of my life and make sure this time it's for good." As he slumped onto the sofa, Nikita stared at Rahul for a few minutes before wiping her tears and running out of the flat. He kept staring at the closed door for what felt like hours, then picked up his phone and dialed Priya's number.

FORTY
SEARCH ON

A loud knocking on the door woke Rahul up. When he checked his watch and saw that it was six in the morning, his drowsiness turned to anger. His anger increased twofold as he opened the door to find Rajeev leaning on it. Before he could say anything, Rajeev barged in, shouting, "Where is she? Nikita! Nikitaaaa! Will you just come out?"

His incessant shouting woke Priya, who came out with an annoyed face and joined them in the hall. This startled Rajeev for a moment, then he turned to grab Rahul by the collar of his T-shirt and screamed in his ear, "What the hell is she doing here? Where is Nikita?"

Rahul pushed him away and freed himself as he replied, "Who knows? She was hiding about you and her, and when she finally confessed, I told her to get out of my life so that you two can live in peace and stop screwing up my life every day. I thought after that she would have run into your arms. You should know where she is! Why are you here screaming? Where did she go?" Rahul was confused and started scratching his head, but Rajeev lost his patience and dashed out of the room before Rahul could finish what he was saying.

Priya came and hugged Rahul, who was engrossed in his thoughts. It took him a moment to come to his senses, and he pushed her back, saying, "I need to find where she has gone. I thought she went back to him after I shouted at her. She hardly has any friends, and I doubt she will take favors from anyone. I am not sure where she found a place to stay on such short notice."

Even after racking his brain for a long time, Rahul couldn't think of a single place she might have gone. He had left immediately to follow Rajeev, silently thanking his instincts for doing so, as Rajeev drove steadily, seemingly knowing exactly where he was headed.

While driving, Rahul also called all their mutual friends and even tried reaching out to a few nearby hospitals, growing increasingly anxious. His thoughts were interrupted when he saw Rajeev's car come to a stop near a secluded apartment building with dilapidated walls. This sight made Rahul's heart sink and filled his mind with questions. Did Rajeev know something about Nikita that he didn't?

He stepped out of his car, seething with anger, and followed Rajeev. Without hesitation, he grabbed Rajeev by the shoulder and forcefully turned him around, demanding, `"How do you know Nikita will be in this place? Are you stalking her or tracking her phone? What have you done?"

Rajeev pushed Rahul back and replied, "You really don't seem in a position to question me after you threw her out of your house and didn't bother to know her whereabouts for so long. If you don't mind, I would like to see Nikita now without you hovering around."

The commotion prompted Nikita to open the door of her apartment. She was surprised to see Rajeev standing there and even more horrified to find Rahul behind him. She blinked twice before asking, "What are you both doing here? Just wait outside. I'll come out. I don't want all your drama to reach my roommates. I live with two other people and don't want to create a scene inside."

Rahul and Rajeev paced around but in opposite directions, giving each other angry looks until Nikita came outside. Rajeev shouted at her, "Are you out of your mind? If this idiot threw you out, then you had to come to me. You can't disappear on me, even if you are angry. You've got to talk to me. What if something happened to you? Where are you staying? I've told you millions of times that you can always use my card and my house. I am always a call away. You don't have to live in a dump hole."

Nikita opened her mouth to speak but closed it immediately as Rahul approached, starting his accusations, "What are you trying to prove? You create this disappearing act to get sympathy and attention. You've always done what you wanted, but now you're trying to act like I forced you to leave. You could have easily stayed in the other flat if you didn't want to go back to Rajeev. What are you trying to prove by living here and portraying yourself as a victim?" Nikita stared at them silently for a long moment before stepping forward. She grabbed Rajeev by the elbow and gently pulled him away from Rahul, saying firmly, "Rahul, I'll talk to you in a moment."

Nikita scratched her chin as she started speaking in a low tone, "I told you that I don't need anything from you. After I had a fight with Rahul, I didn't come back to you because I don't trust you. When you went behind my back to Rahul, it looked more like you manipulated the situation and used it to put down Rahul instead of actually caring about me. You've been doing this since the day we met. I can't play these games anymore. You might want to win something, but I'm looking for a relationship, and I don't find that with someone who is constantly plotting instead of thinking about how to care for me. I'm sure you don't trust me either, which is why you went directly to Rahul to ensure your stand is clear. Anyway, I don't need any explanation or debate on this topic. I'm just done with us. I would like my divorce papers signed."

She saw Rajeev purse his lips in frustration, but before he could speak, she turned towards Rahul. "I wasn't looking for sympathy. I cheated on you and took responsibility for it by getting out of your life. It seemed like you didn't want to know my whereabouts, so I didn't tell you. Issues like where I should live or whether I should have gone to Rajeev or stayed at your flat should not concern you. I won't be troubling you anymore, I promise. The rest is my problem to deal with."

Rahul pulled his hair in frustration and replied, "Your shameless attitude after cheating and hiding the truth from me is unbelievable. It was a mistake to come here. You both deserve each other. Narcissists!"

As she turned away, Rajeev interjected, "I don't get what you are trying to do. You want to prove you can live alone? You want to prove that you don't love me or need me? Fine! Have it your way. I will be there whenever you need me, but I'm done cajoling you now. I'll send the papers to this address. I hope you come to your senses and, whenever you're done with your drama, come back to my house."

As Nikita watched both of their cars leave, she suddenly felt sick and fainted on the road.

FORTY-ONE

A SURPRISE NOT SO PLEASANT

The loud doorbell ruined Rahul's morning once again as he mumbled in his sleep, "Why do people wake up so early?" His frustration grew when he saw Nikita standing at the door. "Why do you and your husband hate my sleep so much that you need to bother me so early in the morning?"

Nikita's eyes widened in surprise as she saw Priya coming out of the bedroom, but she quickly composed herself and said to Rahul in a low tone, "Can we talk somewhere in private?" Rahul glanced back at Priya and replied monotonously, "No. You can say whatever you want in front of her."

Nikita looked at Priya, then stared at Rahul for a moment before shrugging her shoulders. "Fine, I don't care! I'm pregnant. I found out the day you both came to see me. I thought you should know. You can be as involved as you want. I don't expect anything else."

Rahul looked at Nikita speechlessly, his eyes wide open. Before he could say a word, Priya pushed Nikita back and shouted, "Are you serious? This is really low, even for you.

Nice way to swoop into Rahul's life again, but I'm not letting you destroy him one more time. It took him a long time to recover from your betrayal, and now you're here again to disrupt our peace. You just can't stand to see us happy, can you? This is the height of cooking up nonsense stories. Don't try to pass off Rajeev's child as Rahul's."

Nikita looked at Rahul, anticipating a retort, but seeing him cover his face with both his hands, she replied, "I'm not trying to pass off anything. This is just for your information. I'm having Rahul's baby. You both can still be as happy as you want in your Lala land, for all I care." She didn't wait for a response before turning on her heel and storming off.

As Nikita was looking for a cab on the street, she heard commotion behind her and turned to find Rahul stumbling against a parked car as he ran towards her. "What?" Nikita asked, exasperated. Out of breath, Rahul managed to reply, "I want a confirmation test." Nikita gaped at him in shock, then collected herself and replied, "You don't have to bother about it. My mistake was coming here."

Nikita got into an approaching cab and tried to shut the door but Rahul blocked her and managed to sit in the cab as well. "You can't leave after dropping this bombshell. I'm fed up with your lies. I need proof this time, and if you won't agree, I'll go to court. Don't force me to do things I don't want to do." Nikita looked away in disgust as she replied, "I don't know who is more pathetic—you or Priya. She has taught you to speak her language." Nikita sat sullenly, her arms crossed, while Rahul gave the cab driver directions to the hospital.

After finishing her tests with the doctor, Nikita came out to find Rahul sitting outside. Ignoring him, she started moving towards the hospital exit. "Where do you think you're going? You're going to wait until the test results come back. I've spoken to the lab assistant, and they'll try to give them to us today," Rahul said, trying to stop her by holding her elbow. Nikita pulled herself free and replied, "I know the results. You have doubts, so you can stay back for the results. I don't care either way."

After leaving the hospital, Nikita took a cab again to her next stop and sighed as she arrived at Rajeev's house. She gave him a call, and within a few minutes, Rajeev came running to the gate. Before she could say anything, she was engulfed in his bear hug. As Rajeev kept murmuring, "I knew you would come back to me," Nikita pushed him away. She said in a tired tone, "I am not back. Let's go inside. I need to tell you something, and I wanted it to come from me before it gets splashed across the news. I owe you at least that."

As Nikita spoke, she noticed a dejected Rajeev slumping down on his sofa. For a fleeting moment, she considered going over to console him but ultimately decided against it and walked out of the house. While she was still looking around for an auto or cab, Rajeev appeared at the gate, calling her back. He handed her a file and said, "Here are the papers. I've signed them. You'll need them now to marry Rahul."

Nikita paused as she stepped into the cab and replied, "Thanks, but I'm not marrying him. He doesn't even believe it's his child." Rajeev stood frozen, his mouth agape in shock, as the cab sped away, leaving him staring after her.

FORTY-TWO

AN UNHAPPY WEDDING

Nikita woke up to the sound of her roommates screaming in the hall. Annoyed, she got up to shout at them but her annoyance turned to shock. The reason for their screaming was a confused Rahul standing in the hall, looking around skeptically while the two girls pranced around him, trying to take photos. Relief washed over him the moment he spotted Nikita. She went back to her bed with Rahul following behind. As she got back under the covers, she told him, "Those two are huge fans of yours. Before you leave, kindly give them a selfie, or they will die crying."

Rahul sat down on her bed and replied, "They've already taken hundreds of photos. I came to discuss our future plan." Nikita sat up in bed and gave him an annoyed look. "What future plan? You can come to see the baby whenever you want. You don't need a plan for that. It's your child, even if you refuse to accept the fact."

Rahul scratched his forehead and said in a low tone, "I just needed to be absolutely sure. After what you did, you really don't have much ground to show arrogance. I'm not going to apologize for asking for a DNA test from someone who cheated on me, so spare me the morality lecture. Anyway, I don't want to talk about 'us' because there is no more 'us,' but we cannot keep up this senseless fight, at least for the sake of the baby. We also need to discuss how to get our marriage registered, and before that, you'll have to complete your divorce proceedings with Rajeev. So, lots of things to talk about and even more to do. Get dressed; we need to start moving."

Nikita rubbed her eyes and got down from her bed, saying, "Hold your horses for a second. Are you proposing marriage to me in this highly pathetic manner? You haven't even asked me about my divorce. My divorce was just finalized a few days ago. I was going to tell you, but I didn't want to interrupt your cuddling time with Pri."

Rahul got up and held her hand as he spoke angrily, "I am not proposing any marriage. You should be the last person to throw shade about Pri when what you did is way worse. I don't want to talk about these things. I am trying really hard to forget your behavior for the sake of our child. Again, only and only for the sake of our child, we will have a registered marriage in court so that my child is legally and socially accepted by the world. So, we need to work that date out soon. You and your issues can go to hell for all I care, but unfortunately, you carry my child, so I had to swallow my pride and talk to you. I have no interest in any proposal or any marriage with you. Just sign the papers which will confirm that the child is not out of wedlock. You can then go ahead and make a fool of yourself with Rajeev for all I care."

Nikita started laughing as she replied, "Out of wedlock? Are you serious? Since when did you go all traditional after propagating open relationships and what not? I am not marrying someone for the sake of societal norms. I didn't even want to come to you, but just like you, I also only care about our child who should be aware of both his parents. You are a father anyway and can meet whenever you want. We don't have to do this marriage drama just so that you don't lose face in front of your elitist friends and innumerable fans."

Rahul held his head with both his hands in frustration and replied, "You lost your senses long ago when you fell in love with a violent abuser, so expecting any kind of logic from you is useless. Let me make this clear again. Either you get married to me and move into our flat with the child, or I will go to court for full custody. I am not going to meet my kid on weekends after taking permission from you. It shouldn't take a brilliant mind like yours to understand who the judge will favor for custody—a guy who owns two flats and has a flourishing career as a musician, or some girl who is a part-time employee living in a PG shared with two others in a dump of a room. Make a decision by tomorrow, as I am going to arrange the court dates for the marriage, which can also turn into custody battle dates entirely based on your wish."

"Are you threatening me? You cannot force me to marry you," Nikita shouted at Rahul as he was leaving the room. He turned and said, "No threat. No force. You decide. It's me with the baby, or nothing at all." Nikita slumped on the bed in despair, and it was almost an hour before an idea struck her. She picked up her phone to call Priya.

Even before Rahul could open the door of his flat, it was pulled open by Priya, fuming with anger and both her hands were firmly planted on her hips. Rahul was taken aback as she screamed at him, "You are going to marry her? Are you out of your mind? She is using that child to get you back. How can you be so dumb? We don't even know if that child is yours. I will not let you be fooled by her tricks anymore. She has been doing this since time immemorial—lies and lies just to get your sympathy and attention, and you blindly follow her even after knowing her treachery."

Rahul pushed her aside as he sat down on the sofa and laid back his head, saying, "It's mine. I got all the tests done myself. The marriage is just a formality for the sake of my child, so please relax. There will be no other change in my life." Priya stared at him, momentarily at a loss for words. Finally, she walked over and sat down beside him, her anger still evident as she said, "What do you mean nothing will change? How can you even propose marriage to someone without talking to me? You are making me look like a fool in front of everyone."

Rahul gave her a grim look as he replied, "So, your problem is your image. Everything is not about you. You have never bothered about what I want. I am fed up with this facade that you need to create for getting random people's approval. I don't need it. I am done with being a puppet to keep you and Nikki happy. I want to live for myself, for once. So, you both can scream as much as you want, but I am not going to take any more permissions from you or Nikki to do what I want. You can contact your PR to ensure your image is not spoiled, but please get out of my house. I need some peace and quiet in life for at least a few moments."

Priya shook her head in disbelief and tugged at Rahul's arm as he once again closed his eyes, folding his arms tightly across his chest. "I can't believe you are throwing me out. Do you think I am some kind of fool who doesn't understand what is going on? First, you went to propose marriage to Nikki, then you want me out of this house. I am not even sure if this baby drama is real. Maybe it's just a way to get what you always wanted—Nikki back in your life. I am not that easy to get rid of, Rahul. I will make both your and Nikki's lives miserable for this."

Rahul got up in anger and pulled Priya up from the sofa, saying, "You and Rajeev already made my life hell when you planned the suicide drama. I owe you no explanation. For once, I want to do what I feel is right without being manipulated by all of you. I know very well that you have never really loved me, Pri. I'm some kind of trophy for you to display so that people applaud you for winning me. You have never bothered to know what I like, but you always knew how to twist and turn things around to ensure you got what you wanted. I am finally fed up with all your games. For once, I just want to concentrate on one person who has not played with my feelings—my kid. I am not going to let you, Rajeev, or even Nikki stop me from having my child live in this house with me 24/7. Do what you want. Let's see who stops me." The determination in his eyes scared Priya as he all but pushed her out of the flat.

She stood taken aback for a second, then decided to channel her anger toward the right person and dialed Nikita. "Is this why you called me? You knew very well that Rahul would throw me out when I would confront him about marriage and try to stop him. You are highly mistaken if you both think that I am that easy to get rid of. Your plan will never work. You may use your baby to get a fake marriage, but he will never love you. Be assured of that!"

Nikita opened her mouth to retort, but the call was abruptly cut off. She was left with nothing to do but stare helplessly, her last option having failed. After long moments of frustration and pacing around her room, she sat down dejected and picked up her phone to call Rahul. "I am ready," she said.

FORTY-THREE
THE ENDLESS CHARADE

"How many parties do I have to attend?" Nikita asked, removing her jewelry with a sigh. She stared at her reflection in the mirror, dreading the effort it would take to remove her layers of makeup.

Rahul smirked as he sprawled on the bed. "Since when did you start getting bored of drama? You've had plenty of experience—remember those stunts you pulled to make Rajeev jealous using me? This should be a walk in the park for you."

Nikita turned to give him an annoyed look. "When will you stop bringing Rajeev into every conversation? I told you, that chapter is over for me."

Rahul covered his face with a blanket and replied, "I've told you multiple times that these formal parties are just for a few days, and then you don't need to sacrifice anything for me. You can continue your life in that flat, and I'll continue mine here. We only need to talk about our kid and not us. I don't need to know what's going on in your life, and you don't need to know mine."

As Nikita got up to leave and made a face at Rahul, who was pretending to sleep, she suddenly felt dizzy and stumbled towards the bed for support, which woke up Rahul. "Are you alright? I've told you to stay in this flat for the last few days so that at least you can call me if you need something. This is highly idiotic. There are two bedrooms—just stay in one," Rahul said as he picked up Nikita, who had slumped on the bed. "I don't want to hear any argument. I'm moving your stuff here. At least I'll be tension-free if I'm in a nearby room, ready to help if you need anything," Rahul said, caressing her hair as he made her lie down.

Nikita made a face and replied, "What about your girlfriends? What about Pri? What about your bachelor freedom that you wanted?"

Rahul tucked her in but turned around as he left the room, only to say, "We will still be living separate lives. You can learn to deal with it. It's the bare minimum a person should do after they've cheated." Nikita threw a pillow at Rahul as he rushed out of the room.

A few hours later, Nikita woke up to the clattering sound in the kitchen and found a girl awkwardly trying to boil milk while wearing a T-shirt that looked like Rahul's. "Let me help you out. You don't seem to be very good at it," Nikita offered, watching the girl fumble with the milk packet and spill most of it.

"Thanks, I hate cooking, but Rohit said he wanted coffee made by me, so I tried," the girl giggled. Nikita raised her eyebrows in surprise. "His name is Rahul. Don't you at least learn each other's names, even if it is your first date?" The girl was taken aback and started stuttering. "I meant Rahul."

Rahul closed his eyes and pretended to be asleep when he saw Nikita enter the room. She stood near his head. "This is a new low even for you. If you're going to call a random girl to make coffee for you in the morning, at least tell her your correct name. Take your coffee. I sent the girl home with your T-shirt. Do yourself a favor and stick to Pri. At least she knew your name," Nikita said, smiling.

Rahul opened his eyes and gave Nikita an angry look as he got up to leave the bedroom. "Please don't worry about my coffee and the girls in my life."

Nikita followed Rahul to the hall, determined to keep teasing him. "I wish I didn't have to worry if you had tried a little better to make this story believable. Next time, at least call the girl for dinner to make it look like a proper date. Anyway, what's up with Pri? Have you both broken up again?"

Rahul sat down on the sofa and gave Nikita a frustrated look. "What do you want? For your happiness, I will ask Pri to stay in the flat in front of us. Is that okay with you?"

Nikita was about to reply but was interrupted by the doorbell. Before she could open the door properly and say hello, Rahul's mom barged in and rushed to hug Rahul.

"Why didn't you tell me what is happening? Pri told all of us. You don't have to get blackmailed into anything. Our family lawyers will make sure that you get full custody and you don't even have to spend a single day with her anymore," she said, giving a disgusted look to Nikita.

Rahul pulled himself out of his mother's embrace as Nikita put her hands on her hips and looked angrily at both of them. "Mom, no one is blackmailing me. Will you please relax? Since when have you started getting so concerned about my dating life? You need to trust my decisions and not Pri's weird imagination," Rahul said, making his mother sit down on the couch.

Rahul's mother replied without taking her angry glare off Nikita, "I never interfered in your dating life because those random girls left your life faster than they came in, but using a child to blackmail you into marriage cannot be tolerated. I am not going to let you or your money go to such gold-diggers."

Nikita scoffed and charged towards her, only to be stopped by Rahul, who held her back by her waist. He also scolded his mother, "Mom, I am not giving any money to anyone, so no one is a gold-digger here. We are just going to raise a child together and still live our independent lives. This marriage is just to ensure the so-called societal norms are followed for the sake of my child. So, please ignore whatever Pri has fed you and let me handle my life my way - exactly what you've been doing for years. I don't need these weirdly unasked-for motherly concerns, this late in my life."

Rahul's mother refused to let it go and kept taunting Nikita, "Living off someone's money is equivalent to taking money. She easily gets to live in a high-end apartment and spend all your money just by claiming she is having your child. Can't you see through these lies? You should have at least asked our lawyer uncle to draft you a prenup. It is never too late. I will tell him to draw up a contract so that she can't get hold of any of your money."

Rahul pulled at his hair in frustration and replied, "Mom, please! You really need to stop taking news feeds from Pri. The marriage is done, and the baby is happening. End of the story. So, you and Pri can try to relax or at least let me be in peace by staying out of my life. I really don't want to upset my very pregnant wife anymore, so please, Mom, if you don't mind, kindly go to the next-door flat for now. I will come there." Rahul held on to an agitated Nikita as his mother banged the entrance door and left the flat.

Nikita pushed Rahul away and screamed, "I don't need your money. Tell your Pri and your darling mother to burn all your money and smoke it up at their parties for all I care. You forced me to marry you, not the other way around." Before Rahul could reply, she stormed out of the hall towards her bedroom.

As she sat on the bed, clutching the bedsheet in frustration, her phone started beeping with notification messages. "Please call as soon as you get my message. I need your help. Rajeev is not well," read a message from Philip. Nikita clenched and unclenched her fists for a while, then picked up her phone to dial Philip

FORTY-FOUR

RAJEEV'S LIFE CRUMBLES

After a long consoling session with his monther, Rahul was finally able to break free. He sneaked into his flat, trying to reach his bedroom without switching on the lights. As he glanced towards Nikita's room, he found it empty, the bed untouched. Perplexed by her absence at this time of the night, he picked up his phone to call her. Before he could dial the number, he heard the main door open. Moving towards the hall, he found Nikita tiptoeing towards her bedroom. Nikita had to cover her eyes as Rahul switched on the lights.

"So, do I get to know about your night out at least after it's over? I wouldn't have bothered to ask, but unfortunately, my kid has to go on all night outs with you until this pregnancy is over. After my baby is born, you can party with whichever idiot you want, but before that, I want to know my kid's whereabouts," Rahul said, his eyes stern and teeth gritted.

Nikita tried to recover from the sudden blinding lights as she replied, "I went to meet Philip." Rahul shook his head and stepped closer to her, his expression darkening. He placed a hand on the wall for support, leaning in as he asked angrily, "Why? Was it Philip or Rajeev?"

Nikita blinked, staring at Rahul, then tried to move past him towards her room without replying. Rahul grabbed her elbow and pulled her closer, screaming in her ear, "Answer me! If you think you can get away by making me a fool again, then you are highly mistaken."

Nikita brushed off his hand and pushed him away. "It was Philip. He wanted to talk about some issues Rajeev is facing at the office. He's having financial problems and a legal tussle with his own father over his company. So Philip called to tell me all this. I didn't meet or even talk to Rajeev. Happy now?"

"Should I celebrate that you're still so concerned about your ex's personal life? Or should I be ecstatic about the fact that you're planning to meet your ex to solve his issues, the issues in which you have absolutely no expertise? What should I be happy about?" Rahul asked, crossing his arms and speaking in a stern tone.

Nikita shrugged her shoulders and replied, "You can think whatever you want. I told you the truth. I thought we were living our independent lives, so let's stick to the basic rule. You don't question my whereabouts, and I will extend the same courtesy. Deal?"

Rahul threw his hands up in the air in frustration as he said, "Fine, you want to play this game? Let's play! Boy, I can't wait for this kid to be born. The sooner that happens, the sooner I can stop bothering to talk to you. I have never seen a more opportunistic, emotionless person like you." Before Nikita could retort, Rahul went into his room and closed the door with a bang.

Nikita came to her bed and started typing a message as she lay down: "Can we meet tomorrow? I need to talk. Just for a few minutes. I can come to your office." She stared at her phone for a few moments before touching the send button. She finally sent the message and kept staring at the screen, waiting for confirmation that Rajeev had read her message, but she fell asleep before it could happen.

Rajeev read her message first thing in the morning, but it only made him lose his cool. He threw his phone on the bed in frustration. After pacing around to calm his nerves, Rajeev picked up the phone, deleted the message, then went to the washroom and started getting ready for the office.

In the morning, a half-awake Nikita tumbled towards the kitchen to make her coffee, only to find Rahul already cooking there. "Where is my coffee? There was a bottle in the cupboard. Don't tell me that hiding coffee is your new method to annoy me, because even for you, that would be really petty," Nikita asked Rahul after searching around the kitchen for nearly ten minutes.

"I bought a new packet of decaf coffee, so try that. I've also made you some salad and a healthy breakfast instead of those useless sugar-coated corn flakes you eat. You need to eat healthily for my kid, so I will be helping you change your senseless food habits from now on. I've given away most of your unhealthy junk food to our domestic help, and in this kitchen, you will only find healthy options," Rahul said, leaning on the kitchen counter as he lectured Nikita.

"You've got to be kidding me! I will eat what I want to eat. You do know that I can eat anything outside when I go to work, or have you planned to stop that too, being the borderline dictator that you are turning out to be?" Nikita shouted at Rahul and threw the coffee packet at him.

"If you force me to do that, then I will. For now, I plan to stop everything you do that hampers my child's health. I will be visiting the doctor with you every week and closely monitoring your health charts. I've already booked all the appointments and stuck a detailed timetable at our entrance door, so make sure you're ready for that routine too. Keep your Rajeev shenanigans to a limit and come back home on time, or else your work time will also need to be analyzed. I am very serious about my kid, and I suggest you do the same. I have to leave for work as I have some recordings today. See you in the evening."

Nikita picked up a pan nearby and threw it at him, but missed by inches as Rahul ran towards the door.

Nikita had spent the entire day in the office looking at her phone, sending messages to Rajeev, and staring at the screen. It only led to disappointment because she received the read notifications but no reply from him. Determined to see him, she decided to visit Rajeev's office before going home. As soon as she got out of her cab, she saw that the entire floor was dark, except for Rajeev's cabin. It was the only window which had some movement and lighting.

Rajeev dropped the file in surprise as he saw Nikita opening the door. He gave her a stern look and said, "What are you doing here?"

Nikita came in and sat on a chair. "Where is everyone? When I was here, you wouldn't let me leave the office before 9, and now the entire office is gone before 7. I missed seeing this benevolent boss side of yours when I was working here."

"There wasn't much to do. Why are you here? Why have you been messaging me incessantly since last night? If you are stalking me, then it is too late for your love obsession. Your new hubby might have some issues with you standing in front of me at this late hour. Go home. You are pregnant, so you should be resting instead of obsessing over me and my office," Rajeev said, sitting down on his chair across the room.

"I would be resting if you had answered my messages or calls. Philip told me you are having issues with the ownership of the company, and the client feedbacks are not good," Nikita said, tilting her head to gauge Rajeev's expressions.

Rajeev pushed the desk in front of him in anger as he got up and shouted, "Why do you suddenly care? I told you to be with me. I would have been enough for you and your child, but you chose to get married to Rahul. Then why this fake concern for me? Just leave now. I don't have time for you and your drama."

Nikita stood up and shrugged. "I've told you multiple times why I had to marry Rahul, but that doesn't change the fact that I care about you. If you need any help or just an ear to talk to, then call me."

Rajeev kept staring at the wall without turning to look at her. "If you want to help, come into my life fully. It's either Rahul or me. Stop making fools of both of us. You can't float between two boats, so just pick one and leave the other." Nikita left without replying and slammed the door behind her.

Rahul was pacing up and down the apartment when Nikita returned. As soon as he saw her enter, he dashed towards her, held her by the elbow, and made her look at the wall clock forcibly while he spoke through gritted teeth, "Can you see what time it is? Nikki, don't make me repeat myself. You are pregnant, and you need to follow a strict timeline to stay healthy for my child's sake. After the baby is born, you can go jump off a cliff for all I care, but until then, use a little of your brain and be careful. I know it's too much to ask from you, so I'm giving you one last chance. Next time, I will make sure you quit your job and stay home until the delivery. Don't make me do things we both will regret."

Nikita tried to free herself as she replied, "I had some urgent work, and I know how to take care of myself better than anyone. You cannot tell me what to do and what not to do."

Rahul refused to let go of her as he shook her, holding both her arms, and said, "Don't mess with me, Nikki. If anything happens that discomforts my child, you cannot even imagine what I will do to you. You really don't want to see that side of me. I am going to hire a permanent driver for you so that at least someone is with you while you are senselessly partying around."

Nikita made a face as she said, "I wasn't partying. I went to my old office to see Rajeev and how he was doing work-wise, as Philip had informed me about professional issues Rajeev is facing. I talked to him for a few minutes. As usual, he didn't tell me anything, and I came back. That's it."

Rahul dug his fingers into his hair with frustration and said in a very low but determined voice, "I have no idea when this Rajeev chapter will end for you. The day you met that guy, your tiny brain lost all functionality. I don't even want to school you on how toxic that guy is, but at least for my child's sake, try to keep a safe distance from that violent, abusive moron. Anyways, you will have a personal driver from tomorrow who will make sure you are home at the right time. Otherwise, think of work-from-home options. These late nights should stop immediately, especially the Rajeev meet-ups. It should be reduced to zero. I won't say it again."

Nikita gave an annoyed reaction to Rahul and stomped towards her room. As she lay down to sleep, she couldn't help but search about Rajeev's company. There were multiple articles about the father-son tussle for ownership and how that had led to a drop in the company's valuation. After tossing and turning on her bed for hours, Nikita got up and dialed Rajeev's grandmother.

FORTY-FIVE

NEW BORN IN THE HOUSE

"You're ready to pop any minute, and all you care about is Rajeev. I don't understand how the love for an alcoholic, abusive ex-husband can be greater than the concern for the birth of your own child. You need to relax and think about the birth, but all you want is to go and visit Rajeev at this moment. What is wrong with you?" Rahul shouted at Nikita, clutching her arms roughly.

Nikita managed to free herself and sat down, taking deep breaths as she replied, "You are more abusive nowadays. I just wanted to give a call to Philip and ask if Rajeev was doing okay. He has been facing some withdrawal symptoms since he gave up his addictions. His father had basically taken over everything and sent him to rehab. You can at best call him a recovering alcoholic if you want to insult him. Philip is making sure he sticks to his medicines and therapy schedules. I only wanted to know if he is doing fine. I am not going to meet him. So, please relax."

Rahul started packing the overnight bag as he said, "I just, for once, want us to talk only about us and our baby instead of Rajeev and his therapy stories, which have been going on for months. I know you are not so naive that you cannot understand it's just a facade. He went to therapy so he can show his face in the boardroom after the tantrums he threw in front of his clients and employees. It's just a way to get out of the firing range and gather some sympathy before a stakeholder meeting happens, and he is bashed by everyone."

Nikita shook her head in frustration as she moved towards the door to leave, "Let's just go to the hospital. I think it is too much to expect any sympathy from you for a guy who has been fighting with his own family and struggling with addictions. So, we should only focus on the baby and have happy conversations. Right now, more than Rajeev, your attitude is stressing me out."

As the nurse took Nikita towards the delivery room, she asked her, "Can you keep this guy away from the room? I would like to deliver in peace, away from his constant bickering." Rahul kept following them and replied, "Yes, I know you would prefer only Rajeev around you, but whether you like it or not, until the baby comes, you are stuck with me."

As Rahul was arranging things around the room, Nikita was talking to the nurse, "Who do you think is more in love with Rajeev, him or me? Up to this point, who has talked about Rajeev more? You are our neutral judge."

The nurse looked at both of them, shook her head in frustration, and left without a word. Nikita shrugged her shoulders and looked at Rahul, "I hope you didn't annoy her too much, or she might take it out on me later."

It felt like ages, but the magical moment had finally arrived. The endless hours of bickering melted away the instant Rahul held the baby and gently brought her close to Nikita. "Look, Nikki, our daughter!" he said, his voice filled with awe and tenderness.

No words were needed as they locked eyes and instinctively reached for each other's hands. In that moment, they knew their relationship had taken on a new meaning—a bond that now carried a new word: parents. A connection stronger than any argument, one that would endure for a lifetime.

The car ride back was not so quiet either, as their bickering was replaced by the baby's crying and a new topic of contention: "Who should name the baby?" "No offense, Rhea sounds too much like Priya. I am not letting you use my daughter to commemorate your ex, present, or future, whatever she is supposed to be," Nikita said, resting in the front seat with her eyes closed but still blabbering about the name given by Rahul.

Rahul opened the flat and held the door open so that Nikita could go in with the baby, saying, "Pri is nowhere in my life. I am not calling her butler every day to know about rehab stints and family issues. I am not messaging obsessively to check if she is financially, mentally, and physically fit. I am also not in constant touch with her grandmother to know about her whereabouts when she refuses to reply to my messages."

Nikita turned to give an angry stern look to Rahul as she replied, "I didn't message Rajeev's grandmother when he didn't reply. I only messaged to check on her and her health. She told me about Rajeev voluntarily. You are just jealous that my name choice of Akriti is way better than yours."

"On a serious note, we can keep a full-time governess if you want. It will be easier for me so that she can travel with me to my shoots and recordings. You also will be free to do your work or stalk Rajeev, whichever one is your priority," Rahul said as he took the baby from Nikita's arms.

Nikita rolled her eyes as she replied in an angry tone, "I am not stalking anyone and we don't need a governess. I fail to understand why a newborn baby has to travel to random places with you and get prone to a million diseases when she can peacefully sleep at home. Who is obsessive now?"

Rahul went into the bedroom and put the baby down with Nikita closely following on his heels. As he tried to put the baby to sleep, he replied in a low tone, "My child will be with me 24/7. I am taking a break for a few months except for some urgent commitments. Either you agree to a governess, or you can travel with me, as my baby will not leave my sight even for a second."

Nikita raised her eyebrows and went to sleep near the baby as she said, "It will be very difficult to do two jobs—playboy and obsessive father. However, it will be fun to watch how you try to score with your millions of girlfriends with a crying baby at arm's distance." Rahul ignored Nikita and concentrated on making the baby sleep. Little did he know that cradling his baby to sleep was going to become a constant routine of his life, something that he would never be bored or tired of doing.

The six months flew by in a whirlwind of chasing after the baby. They divided the chores and often fought over who got to spend more time with their daughter. However, this shared love for their child also highlighted the cracks in their relationship. The constant arguments and underlying distrust only deepened the growing gap between them, with no resolution in sight.

Nikita couldn't find the baby around when she got up in the morning. As she looked around the flat frantically, she saw Rahul open the door with a pram in hand. She started screaming at a surprised Rahul in anger, "Where do you take Niharika without telling me?"

"You were sound asleep, and I didn't want to disturb your rest day," Rahul replied, gently rocking Niharika in his arms as he tried to calm her. "Anyway, we went to the grocery store to pick up some diapers for her."

Suddenly, a girl rushed inside the flat saying, "You left your bag in my car." Nikita stared at the girl and then looked at Rahul with an increasingly piercing gaze and finally said, "It takes a special kind of guts and absolute shamelessness to use your daughter to get a date, that too in the morning. Bravo for the effort."

Before Rahul could reply, the unknown girl chimed in, "Hey, I'm not his date. I was just helping him out — he had so many bags, so I gave him a lift. It didn't look like he had any help, let alone a wife; otherwise, I wouldn't have been here. It's my fault, please don't have any misunderstanding between you both because of me."

Nikita gave a smirk as she replied, "Oh no, you didn't think that a guy with a baby in his arms can have a wife. Must be too much thinking to do for your non-existent brain. Thanks a lot for your help and in case you still want to try your luck with him, then leave your phone number. Otherwise, please scuttle off." Rahul got up in a rush and took the girl outside before Nikita could think of scratching the girl's eyes out.

He came back to find Nikita trying to put Niharika to sleep. He waited for a few moments and then signaled Nikita to follow him outside to the hall so as not to disturb the baby.

He could not control himself any longer and as soon as Nikita entered the room, he burst out, "I have told you multiple times over these last six months that Niharika stays with me at all times. I don't care what issues you have, Nikki. If you want to be in Niharika's life, you can stay here. If you think something else, like Rajeev, is more important, then decide accordingly. Even before our marriage, I made it clear that my kid stays with me at all times. You can adjust your life accordingly and make the choice. The door is always open, but don't even try to question my time with Niharika."

"I don't understand your behavior. She is my daughter too. You can't dictate my time with her," Nikita screamed at Rahul. Rahul went inside to check if Niharika was asleep and came back to hold Nikita roughly by her shoulders as he said, "Keep your voice down. You know very well who will lose if you decide to play a custody battle with me. This is a pretty decent way out that I have offered you. You can have Niharika anytime I am busy with work or on a date. So, spare me this outrage and concentrate more on Niharika than planning a custody fight with me. I might go on a date with the girl you practically threw out moments ago, so tonight Niharika is all in your care. Enjoy."

Nikita brushed off his hands with full force, her eyes blazing with anger as Rahul left the room to check on Niharika again. She stood there, fuming, her gaze fixed on the doorway he had just exited through.

FORTY-SIX
PRIYA TRIES A COMEBACK

Nikita was scrolling through cake pictures when she noticed Rahul on the floor, teaching Niharika how to crawl. She said, "If you have time for that, can you focus on her birthday party as well? Your mom must be expecting something fancy for Niharika's birthday party, and I can't even finalize a cake. I don't want her to get embarrassed in front of her high society friends and then take it out on me."

Rahul picked up Niharika and started rolling her over to make her laugh. "I never had time for her stupid parties. I would rather play with my kid all day than attend her social gatherings. I suggest you ignore her too, like I have been doing for years. I can give you tips on it since I have years of experience behind me."

Nikita got up to open the door as she heard the doorbell but was still not done with Rahul. "Yes, but she loves you and, for her, you can do no wrong. She already hates me, and I don't want to give her one more reason to increase that hatred."

"I don't think anyone hates you more than me. Do you both keep talking about me when I am not here? That is so endearing," Priya said gleefully as she entered the flat. Nikita looked at Rahul with a questioning look and raised eyebrows, which made Rahul get up from the floor in a hurry. He picked up Niharika and put her in the stroller before marching towards Priya.

"Pri, why are you here?" Rahul asked, looking sheepishly at Nikita's angry face. Priya came near to check on Niharika and said, "Your mom called me to organize her granddaughter's birthday party. She's fully convinced that her talentless daughter-in-law will throw a classless, embarrassing party that her social circle will remember for ages."

Nikita crossed her arms and gave a menacing glare to Rahul, which made him pull Priya toward the door. "Look, Pri, tell Mom that we are not throwing any grand party, and none of her friends are invited. So, she need not worry about any embarrassment." This made Nikita throw a few cushions at him and shout, "Let her throw whatever party she wants. I don't care."

Priya pulled her hand from Rahul's grasp and moved toward Nikita, saying, "Good for you. I'm sure you'll be busy stalking Rajeev, so you won't have time to prepare for a birthday party. I met Rajeev the other day. He looked quite disheveled and was telling me about what his father has done and how he's building up his own company again. He also mentioned how much you've been harassing him with your daily texts and calls, which he chooses to avoid since he has enough drama in his life. I didn't know that you still wanted Rajeev in your life. So basically, you can't even get one guy to like you back despite your desperate attempts to cling to all of them. First Rahul, then Rajeev. Is there a third target in mind? Because the first two seem to have no interest in you."

Nikita clenched her teeth, grabbed Priya by her dress, and pushed her against the wall. "Stay away from Rajeev," she hissed. "I'm not joking, Pri. If I find out you've met him again, I will make sure you regret it for the rest of your life. I don't want you anywhere near Rajeev. Drill that into your empty skull and remember it. He has enough issues without you adding to them."

Rahul tried to free Priya from Nikita's grasp, but Nikita refused to let go. She continued in a menacing tone, "Stick to your birthday and marriage parties, but stay away from Rajeev. Don't mess with me, Pri. If you do, it will be the last mistake you make."

Nikita pushed Priya aside, picked up Niharika from her stroller, and took her into the bedroom. Priya adjusted her dress, trying to catch her breath. She screamed at Rahul, "Look at her! I told you she was psychotic. You brought this depraved case into our lives, and she's destroyed all of us. She's not normal. She'd kill me one day. I'm not organizing any birthday party for your kid. I don't want to be anywhere near her. I will tell your mom what kind of nut job her daughter-in-law is. This is the girl you chose over me. Well, you just proved you're dumber than I thought. You totally deserve her."

Rahul rubbed his forehead in frustration as he replied, "Pri, I have told you several times to stay away from us, but you still come up with a lame excuse like a birthday party to waltz back into our lives. Nikki or no Nikki, you would never come back into my life after the suicide stunt you pulled. I don't trust you, and I don't think I ever will. So, choosing you was completely out of the question. We were done long ago, and it has nothing to do with Nikki and everything to do with you. You have always lied to me since school, Pri. How could you ever think we'd end up together? I was always a trophy boyfriend for you, and unfortunately for you, you could never manage to date anyone more famous than me. You're just like my mom, caring more about social status and less about me."

Priya tried to hold Rahul's hand as she stuttered to give an explanation, but Rahul shook his head and moved back, signaling her to leave the house. As she rushed out crying, Rahul sighed and went back into Nikita's room.

FORTY-SEVEN
THE FINAL DEAL

Rahul walked into the room and found Nikita gently feeding Niharika, her soft humming helping their daughter drift off to sleep. When she turned to glance at him, she noticed a grin stretching from ear to ear on his face. "Why are you so happy?" she asked, raising an eyebrow. "I didn't know Pri could have such a positive effect on anyone."

Rahul chuckled and signaled for her to join him on the couch. "Come here," he said, his voice warm yet mysterious, leaving her curious about what had him in such high spirits.

Rahul started playing with Nikita's hair as she sat down, "In nearly two years of our marriage, we haven't had much of a married life. We've fought day in and day out. There hasn't been a single day that we've actually talked as husband and wife, let alone been civil to each other, at least as old friends. There is no love lost between us, and our marriage is a joke. I brought random dates home just to irritate you, and I am sure you talked to Rajeev and his family non-stop just to annoy me."

Nikita pulled herself back and gave Rahul a skeptical look. "Why are you being so emotional? Did Pri say something again? Look, if she wants to throw some birthday party, I'm fine with it. I don't care anymore. Just keep her out of my sight, and she can do whatever she wants. I don't want to give unnecessary importance to her existence in my life."

Rahul smiled and cupped Nikita's face with both his hands as he replied, "That's the point, baby, that's the whole point. You don't care about Pri anymore. You didn't care about any of those girls I brought here to get a tiny reaction of jealousy from you. You only care about one person, which you proved by pouncing on Pri and giving her a near-death experience just because she talked to Rajeev. I'm scared to think what would have happened if she had touched him."

Nikita suddenly got up and started fiddling with her fingers in nervousness as she replied, "What are you talking about? Why would I be jealous of anyone? I don't have any right to stop you from doing anything. That's what we decided before marriage. I cheated on you, so I'm the last person who should expect any loyalty from you. I'm thankful that you decided to give a normal family life to Niharika. I don't want to ruin anything by being jealous. You hated my possessive, clingy nature even when you were dating Pri, so I didn't want to bring all that back and ruin everything for Niharika."

Rahul got up and held her arms, replying with a smile, "I guess that's what's missing. Your natural possessiveness, which you used to have for me, has now shifted to Rajeev. Infact it has even increased tenfold. Your jealousy used to be visible with Pri before, even when you tried hard to hide it. The same jealousy I saw again today. You weren't hiding it until now, Nikki. You just weren't feeling any jealousy. You felt it today after months when Rajeev's name came up.

Then you could no longer control your real feelings. Your epic outburst was a scene to watch."

Nikita shook her head in frustration, "What are you trying to prove? That I'm in love with Rajeev and I'm lying to you? I've told you thousands of times: that chapter of my life is closed, and I only want to concentrate on Niharika."

Rahul sat down on the bed again and covered his eyes with both hands in frustration, replying, "Trust me, no one would be happier than me if that chapter of your life were closed. We both need to think about what we want and what we should do to make our miserable life bearable so that Niharika stays away from this chaos. Right now, the betrayals and heartbreaks are making it difficult for me to act normal in front of Niharika. All I can think of is how my life was peaceful and happy before Rajeev came and bombarded everything. Since childhood, I had imagined Nikki and Rahul would be together forever, where you would listen to all my senseless talks, and I would tolerate all your shenanigans. However, the reality in the name of Rajeev hit me too hard. I need to wrap my head around this truth. I suggest you do the same so that we can decide on how to coexist peacefully for Niharika's sake. Seeing a lovestruck wife obsessed with her ex-husband every day is becoming unbearable for me."

As Rahul stepped out of the room, Nikita remained seated in silence, her mind racing. After a few moments, she abruptly stood up, determination flashing in her eyes. Grabbing her purse, she dialed for a taxi and headed toward the door.

Rahul caught sight of her slipping out quietly. His shoulders tensed, and frustration boiled over. Without thinking, he turned and slammed his fist against the wall, the dull thud echoing his inner turmoil.

Rajeev was half-asleep when he got a call from his door security team informing him that Nikita was there. He got up in surprise and told them to let her in as he quickly dressed. As Nikita walked across the hall, she pursed her lips and fiddled with her fingers nervously. Her anxiety increased as soon as she saw Rajeev enter the hall.

"What are you doing here this late? Are you okay?" Rajeev asked, noticing Nikita looking down, standing awkwardly with one foot over the other. After a long silence, Nikita managed to mutter, "I don't know why I am here."

Rajeev sighed and gently pulled Nikita toward the living room sofa, making her sit beside him. "I didn't respond to your messages because I knew you were already getting updates about me from Philip," he said softly. "I didn't want to be directly in touch with you because I didn't want to spoil your relationship with Rahul more than I already have. In fact, I'm not even sure how Rahul will react if he finds out you're here. I don't blame him; it would drive me crazy if I were in his place."

Nikita closed her eyes as she lay back on the sofa and replied, "I have no idea what to do. Pri came today and told me she met you. It made me so angry that you were sharing your issues with her while you won't even message me. I don't know how I will manage if you actually get close to someone. I think I will lose my mind. Rahul saw how I reacted and said I was still not over you. I want to be over you. I want to forget you. I only want to think about Niharika and nothing else. I was doing fine until Pri came waltzing into my life and started boasting about being your confidant. I felt like punching her. Two years of effort put into forgetting you was all down the drain. I have given up and come to you for a solution. You used to make everything so easy for me, so just solve this problem too."

Rajeev smiled as he got up and started pacing around while speaking, "I wish I had a solution; then I could have made my life simpler too. Let's just try to solve your main trouble. I won't talk to Pri again or any other girl about my personal problems. No more dates, marriage, girls—what else?"

Nikita opened her eyes and made a face, giving him an annoyed look as she replied, "Stop kidding. It's your life. You can do whatever makes you happy. You don't need to make sacrifices for anyone."

Rajeev smiled and came near, touching her head with his as he said, "This would make me happy—seeing you happy. I have lost a lot of things in life recently and don't want to lose you too. I am here for you for life, so just name what you want, and I will try to get it for you."

Hearing these words, Nikita smiled and suddenly turned to give him a hug. Before Rajeev could process what had happened or even move his hands to hug her back, Nikita pulled away and ran out of the house. As soon as she reached home, she jumped out of the cab and raced to her flat with the same speed. She was panting when she finally entered her house and went to Rahul's room.

"What is wrong with you?" Rahul asked as he handed her a glass of water and signaled for her to remain calm as Niharika was sleeping. Nikita, still catching her breath, waved her hand dismissively and gestured toward the living room. "Come out here," she said between gasps, her voice urgent but firm.

Rahul followed reluctantly, giving her a questioning side glance. His brows furrowed as he leaned against the wall, tilting his head slightly. "Have you completely lost your mind? What's going on? Why are you so excited and out of breath?"

Nikita couldn't control her happiness and her words tumbling out like a long-held confession. "You asked me what happened to me suddenly when we both were so happy as friends since childhood. Well, I finally realized what happened. For the first time, someone saw the mess behind my possessiveness—my obsession—and didn't shrink away with judgment or call me embarrassing, but simply accepted me as I am, flaws and all. Someone who understood my emotions because he was just as jealous and possessive of me."

Her eyes sparkled with a newfound clarity as she continued, "He understood my madness and was equally crazy. With him, I didn't have to control my behavior or force myself to meet society's so-called standards for being classy and ladylike. I could finally be me—without him being ashamed of who I was or how I acted."

She took a deep breath, her tone softening but remaining firm. "I've found someone with whom I can be my true self, without needing to fit into your or Pri's rigid norms of what's acceptable. And that, Rahul, is what changed everything."

Nikita whirled around the hall as she exclaimed, "I don't want to behave maturely or curb my jealousy just to make you or your mother feel comfortable or unembarrassed by me. I was always your second choice, Rahul. Always in the background, while Pri was the front-end display—your trophy girlfriend."

She took a step closer, her tone intensifying. "But with him? I'm his first choice. He's crazy possessive over me, to the point of being dangerously stalkerish, and you know what? I feel the same way about him. I don't have to tone myself down or pretend to be someone I'm not. He accepts my madness because he's just as mad about me."

Her voice broke slightly, but she held her ground. "I'm done being a backup. I deserve someone who obsesses over me the way I obsess over them. And that's not you."

Rahul smiled as he stopped Nikita from dancing around the hall and held her closer, saying, "It's funny how you made me fall for you, all the while you were falling for someone else. While I was stupidly in love with you, you had already become head over heels for someone else."

Nikita pulled away and tried to retort, but Rahul raised his hand to stop her from talking and continued, "I'm glad you've realized you're in love because I want you to feel the same misery I've been feeling all these years. I want you to feel the same pain and suffocation of being in love with someone and being able to do nothing about it. I will not divorce you, and there will be no shared custody. Let's make a deal to be miserable together. You have to choose between Rajeev and Niharika. You living with a recovering addict won't look good in a custody battle, and I'll make sure it turns ugly, so make your choices wisely. If I'm not getting my love, then I can't stand to see other lovebirds flying either. Let's share the misery together."

Rahul stared at her, his eyes lacking any expression as he tapped her cheeks softly and turned to return to his bedroom. Nikita slumped down on the couch, covering her face with both hands as tears streamed down her cheeks, whispering his words, "LET'S SHARE THE MISERY TOGETHER."

Author's Note

Thank you for taking the time to journey with me through these pages. I hope this story sparked something inside you—whether it was a smile, a tear, or a reflection. Until we meet again in another story.

Ekta

About The Author

Ekta's childhood love for reading fiction novels translated into her passion for storytelling and literature, eventually leading her to pursue a career as an author with a particular focus on writing fiction. Her work is profoundly influenced by the stories and books she cherished during her formative years.